OUR WILD BRIDE

LACEY DAVIS

Can They Tame Their Wild Bride or Will She Rebel and Leave Them?

Blanche Underwood earned her reputation when she was twelve. Now, six years later, with the death of her father and the loss of her family ranch, she's destitute. And no man in Charleston wants to marry her. They're afraid of her hellacious ways. And she's certainly not a lady. Can the town matchmaker find someone willing to take a chance?

Martin Sanders and Jakob Moore have been friends for twenty years, starting the Double M Ranch. Now, Jakob wants a proper, chaste wife while Martin just wants their ranch to be the successful endeavor that would make his dead parents proud.

Can they claim the wild Blanche and teach her to be the wife they need or will her rowdy behavior devastate their hopes and dreams?

CHAPTER 1

*B*lanche Underwood grabbed her rifle, opened the window, and watched as the riders approached her home. Damn, damn, and double damn. It was that fella that her papa had lost the ranch to in a card game, and this time it appeared he looked serious as he had brought the sheriff with him.

For months now, she'd resisted him.

Knowing it wasn't in her better interest, but unable to stop herself, she aimed the rifle and pulled the trigger. The bullet landed right in front of the new owner's horse and he had to fight to control the animal. Loud cursing filled the air.

"Serves you right for stealing my ranch," she said, pushing her red hair out of her face.

It wasn't fair. This was her home, and her father had not only lost it in a card game, but then he had the audacity to die, leaving her alone. What was she going to do?

The sheriff continued toward the house. She knew

better than to shoot at a lawman. Why had the new owner brought him out?

When the sheriff's horse reached the house, he stared up at her through the window. She lowered her rifle and met him on the porch, wearing her pants and shirt. Skirts were beautiful, but they didn't fit the lifestyle of a rancher.

They were cumbersome and no one could exactly call her a lady.

"Miss Underwood, that wasn't right."

"I'm just trying to keep vermin away from the ranch," she said, pulling her shoulders back and narrowing her eyes at the man, her trusty rifle by her side.

The man who claimed he owned the property rode up beside the sheriff.

"Sheriff, I've been a patient man," he said, glaring at Blanche. "But enough."

"It's not your property," she hissed.

The man held up the piece of paper that he claimed her father had signed.

"That's your father's X right there, and witnessed by Brent Harvey," he yelled.

"Brent Harvey is a liar and a cheat," she said, her voice rising. "Anyone could've put that mark there. Even *you*."

How many times was this man going to come out here and claim the land was his? She didn't believe him. It couldn't be true. And yet, she didn't have a good feeling about this little visit.

When the sheriff got involved, it wasn't good.

"Miss Underwood, you have no choice," the sheriff said. "Today is the twenty-seventh, and I expect you to be out of the house by the first. Mr. Jones will take possession then, and if that means I have to haul you out the door, then that's what I'm going to do."

Rage filled her, and she knew she was at the end of her rope. She'd run out of options, and while she could get a lawyer and take the man to court, she had no money. They all knew she was as poor as they came.

After all, she was but a woman trying to survive in a man's world.

And her big, beautiful house sat on one hundred acres of farmland perfect for cotton growing. Plus, a hundred head of cattle and twenty horses that were pure breeds. At one time, this land had been profitable, before her papa found himself at the bottom of a whiskey bottle.

Life wasn't fair. She'd done nothing to deserve this.

Reaching for her rifle, she lifted it up and aimed. "Get the hell off my ranch. It's still mine until the first. Get off now, both of you."

The sheriff shook his head. "Blanche, I know this is not the news you wanted to hear, but I have no choice. I suggest you pack a bag and get going."

But that was the problem. Where would she go? Her father was dead, she had no idea where her mother was, or if she was even still alive, and no brothers or sisters. Her nearest relative was in Texas, and they didn't want her. She had no place to go and now she was losing her birthright.

With Papa's death and the loss of the ranch, she had nothing left worth living for.

"Get out," she yelled. "I've still got three days. Get off my property, now."

She fired the gun into the air and the chickens squawked and ran from the yard.

The sheriff's face turned red. "I should arrest you. But I'm going to leave, but we'll be back on the first. Be gone before then."

She was out of time. This time the ranch would no longer be hers.

As soon as they turned and rode away, tears flowed down her cheeks. Sinking onto the steps, she laid her rifle down and began to cry. Great big hulking sobs.

What was she going to do?

Rusty, her old hound dog, came up beside her and licked her arm and wedged his way to her face where he gave her another lick. She raised her head and glanced out from the only home she'd ever known while she petted her sweet boy. What would she do with him? She couldn't keep him.

Looking out at the pastures, she saw the cattle and the horses and her heart cringed. As much as she hated Mr. Jones, he was going to hate her even more.

She had three days. Three days to sell everything she could. And then she didn't know what she would do.

Going into the house, she packed a suitcase of everything she wanted to keep. Glancing around the home, she knew there was so much she couldn't take with her. Grandma Edith's rocking chair. Her mother's spindle. Her father's...

Damn him.

It was so hard not to feel anger at what he'd done. For years, she'd tried to get him to quit gambling, but he refused. Somehow that bastard Jones had tricked him; she just knew it.

She started to make piles of the things in the house. Items to sell, items to burn, items she couldn't live without.

It took her the rest of the day to get everything organized and part of the next day to get the animals ready.

Then she went into town and hung posters of the big sale out at the Underwood Estate. Everything must go.

As she was hanging a poster on a building, she saw another woman doing the same.

"Hello," she said, glancing over at the woman. "What's this?"

"I'm a marriage matchmaker," the woman said. "I'm looking for girls to travel to Montana where there are eligible men looking for wives."

Blanche glanced at the poster again. "Good men?"

"Why, yes, and if you're not happy there, they will pay your way back to Charleston."

"Humph," Blanche said. What did she have here to return to?

"What kind of men are they?"

"Businessmen, ranchers, bankers, mine owners, all kinds of different men," the lady said, glancing at her. "Are you interested?"

Ranchers. There were ranch owners in Montana looking for a wife. She could live on a ranch, but in Montana, not the hellhole piece of plantation she owned in South Carolina.

Which was no longer hers.

No man around here was going to marry her. Her reputation as a wild woman was widespread, and yet, she hadn't really done anything. Only not been a woman who went to tea parties and acted all refined. A southern belle. A lady – oh no, not her.

No, she wore men's clothes, rode horses astride, cursed, and shot a gun better than any man she knew. And if she wanted, she could outdrink a man too.

But that would never get her married. If she went to Montana, she would need to learn to comport herself like a lady, whether she wanted to or not.

"If I signed up for this matchmaking in Montana, would you teach me how to be a proper lady?"

The woman smiled at her. "I'd do my best."

"When are you leaving? I'm not going to have a place to stay after tomorrow," she said, hoping that with the sale, she would have enough money to hold her over.

"I need three more girls and then we leave. But you're welcome to stay at my place until then," the lady said.

What should she do? Then it hit her. Mr. Jones may have won the ranch in a card game, but he only won the land.

Tomorrow night after she sold all the animals and the furnishings in the house, she'd have a big ol' cookout. She'd leave him with the land and that was it.

She was going to have a fire sale. Everything must go, including herself.

"Count me in," she said. "I'll see you on the first."

CHAPTER 2

*B*lanche had never done anything as hard as what she was about to do. First, choosing what to take and what to sell had been difficult. Getting rid of the cattle, the horses, and even the dog she'd had since she was twelve. How could she go off and leave him, and yet, she knew taking him was not an option.

A kid who lived on the farmland next to theirs had agreed to take him in. Tonight, she was planning on holding him until it was time to say good-bye. And even then, she knew it would be the most difficult thing she'd ever done.

"Come on, Rusty, we have things to do," she said, walking out to the barn. The stalls were empty. She'd even given away the barn cat, Misty.

Glancing around, she looked at the place where she'd learned to ride. Where she'd watched her first colt come into this world. There were so many memories.

With a sigh, she poured lantern fluid around the empty

old building. It was midnight and she hoped no one was awake at this hour. Tears flooded her eyes and she almost couldn't do it. If they had not cheated her father out of the farm, she would never have done this, but cheaters deserved what she was about to do.

Striking a match, she dropped the flame onto the kerosene and with a poof, the flame took off. The leftover hay in the loft sizzled as it caught fire. Mr. Jones was not going to get much.

Stepping back, she watched the old barn go up in flames. The heat from the blaze was intense as she watched it burn.

A pile of furniture lay in the yard. Things she had been unable to sell. Quickly, before she changed her mind, she set fire to things she'd grown up with. Her old doll bed. The toys she'd hoped to hand down to her children. The family items she could not take.

Turning, she walked over to the house and gazed up at the old structure. Home.

No matter what, she couldn't do it. This was the place she'd grown up, and even though she hated Mr. Jones, it would always be her home.

One more night and then it would no longer be hers.

Stepping inside, she leaned down and rubbed Rusty behind the ears. Sinking down onto the floor, she leaned back against the wall. Everything was gone. The house was empty.

The sale had netted her over two thousand dollars. The only thing left on the land was the house.

"You know I'd take you with me if I could," she said,

pulling the dog into her lap. "But I can't. So Elton Smith is going to take good care of you. He promised me he would give you a happy home."

The dog licked her hand and snuggled up against her. He'd been with her through her father's death, the announcement she'd lost the house and land, through everything but her mother's leaving.

Her heart was heavy, and yet she knew that tonight she could not sleep. This was the last night in her home, the last night with her dog. The last night before her life started anew.

When the sky began to turn pink, she took Rusty outside, and sitting together on the old house's porch, they watched as the sun rose. One last sunrise together.

She loaded her carpet bag onto the last horse, which she would sell once she got to town. The buyer would be there waiting for her. In her men's clothing, she climbed up and began to ride away.

"Come on, Rusty," she said her voice breaking. "It's time to go."

The old dog followed her one last time.

Nothing would ever be the same and she knew she would never ever let a man be in charge of her destiny again.

Even if he was her husband.

CHAPTER 3

*B*lanche watched Mrs. Newton walk slowly and carefully with a book on her head. They were working on Blanche's movements. She rushed into a room, her steps determined, knowing where she was going, and not letting anything get in her way.

Not the movements of a true lady.

When she had arrived at the house yesterday, the first thing Mrs. Newton had done was make her bathe and change from her men's clothing into a dress the matchmaker had given her. She'd also been given women's undergarments.

Those damn garments were torture devices that made her lady parts lift up and suck in. She hated the corset and would love to take it out and use it for target practice. But she was trying to change and she had to accept the new rules.

Her papa had never bought her anything that looked like what Mrs. Newton had given her. Sure, he bought her dresses with petticoats, but she only wore them on special occasions. No sense in ruining them while she worked on the farm.

The farm…tears welled in her eyes and she quickly swiped them away. She must concentrate on the here and now and not on what she'd lost. Besides, old man Jones must have shit his pants when he arrived to take over. Nothing left but the land and the house.

"Now it's your turn," Mrs. Newton told her. "Remember, you are a lady. Ladies glide across the room. It should look like you're walking on air."

Like that was possible.

With a sigh, Blanche stood and Mrs. Newton arranged her skirts. She pulled her shoulders back and lifted her chin. Remember, glide…

"Ready?"

"Yes," Blanche said, feeling so uncomfortable. Stiff.

Mrs. Newton placed the book on the top of her head.

"Walk across the room slowly like you're dancing."

"Never been to a dance," she said, thinking that her father had kept her from so many things. Even though he'd gone out to the saloon in town plenty of nights. Gambling their life away.

The thoughts caused her to glance down at her feet and the book tilted and landed on the floor.

Giggles could be heard in the background. She whirled around to see who was laughing at her. If it was Alice Burns, she would take her down and pummel her beautiful face with her fists.

The girl had been her archenemy since grade school

when she tormented Blanche for not having a momma. Though she herself did not have a father.

"Girls," Mrs. Newton admonished, "go to your rooms."

"Blanche, let's start again. I want you to walk across the room five times without losing the book before we move on to your next lesson."

She hoped to hell the next lesson was not as tedious as this one. But she got the feeling that none of this was going to be easy.

Mrs. Newton pulled her shoulders back and tilted her chin up and then the hated book was placed on her head. Glide slowly...

"Again," she said.

Blanche began to walk, carefully keeping the book on her head. She made it across the room four times when she heard Alice's voice.

"She has no momma. It's whispered that her mother ran out on her and her trashy father. Took off with the pan salesman."

The woman was deliberately trying to make Blanche angry and it was working. Fury spread through her as the girl told her malicious gossip. She felt the book wobble. One more pass and then she would beat the hell out of her.

"I hear she's just like her tramp of a mother. It must be passed down," Alice said loud enough for Blanche to hear her.

Mrs. Newton shook her head and Blanche knew she also heard Alice's voice.

When she finished the fifth lap across the room, she removed the book and handed it to Mrs. Newton. Then she walked into the hallway and grabbed Alice by the front of her dress, bringing her up close to her.

"One more word and that pretty nose of yours will be crushed. Do you understand me?"

The girl's blue eyes widened with fear.

"You may have gotten away with tormenting me in school, but it's not going to be so easy here. I will kick your ass all the way down the street after I break your nose so that no man will look twice at you. Do you understand me?"

"Girls," Mrs. Newton said, coming between the two women. "Alice, that was uncalled for. You deliberately baited Blanche. Go to your room. One more incident like this and you'll be staying in Charleston. Do you understand?"

"Yes, ma'am," she said, straightening her dress and giving Blanche a mean, disgusted glance.

Then Mrs. Newton turned and glared at Blanche. "We were doing so well. Your conduct and your threats are not ladylike. Do not let me hear them again or you will be staying in Charleston. Now back to work. The rest of you, practice your needlepoint. Stay in your rooms, until we are done."

The women scattered and Blanche sighed. She couldn't afford to lose this opportunity. She wanted to get to Montana and find herself a rancher for a husband.

"I'm sorry, but she has tormented me since I was a child. I will no longer accept her saying horrible things about my mother or me."

Mrs. Newton stared at her. "How do you think a lady would respond to her?"

"I don't know. All I know is how to use my fists. That's what I was taught."

The woman smiled. "And now you're going to learn a new way. Sit down and let's practice."

What were they going to practice? What other way was there?

"Have you heard about Blanche's mother?"

Her spine stiffened and she felt her fingers clench.

Mrs. Newton took her hand. "Now say something nice back to me."

Confusion filled her as she tried to remember what she'd been taught about her mother.

"I heard that she was beautiful. Papa said she had the sweetest laugh. He missed her right up until the day he died."

She squeezed her hand. "Perfect. Not only did you respond in kind, but you gave us new information that we didn't know about your mother."

"But it's hard to think that way when someone is taunting you."

"Yes, it is. Let's try again," she said.

Blanche just wanted to get up and run down the hall and pound Alice, but she knew that was not in her best interest.

"Did you hear that Blanche is taking after her mother?"

She licked her lips. Was it true? Could she be taking after her mother? Papa always said she looked just like her.

"My papa said I look just like my mother. That sometimes I would say something and it sounded just like her. But I don't want to be her."

Was that a good thing? All she knew about her mother was that she had run away with the pan salesman, leaving Blanche behind. And even now that hurt.

"Excellent," Mrs. Newton told her. "This is not going to be easy. And knowing Alice Burns, she will try to start trouble again. Prove to me that your lessons are working. Show me that you're a lady by responding not with your fists, but your words."

Blanche wasn't certain she could keep her fists from exploding on the woman, but she had to try.

"I'll do my best."

"Good, now let's practice the art of serving tea. The last girl arrives next week and we'll be leaving shortly thereafter."

A tingle of fear spiraled up her spine. Could she go off and leave the only place she'd known? Did she really have any choice?

CHAPTER 4

"Blanche, I need your help," Daisy whispered standing close to her.

Daisy was one of the nicer girls and she'd helped Blanche adjust to living among the women. She was kind and friendly and Blanche knew Daisy also had no choice but to leave Charleston.

"What do you need?"

"Not here," Daisy said, glancing at the other young women who sat around crocheting or doing needlework. They all looked like such perfect young women, but most of them had a past. Most of them were hiding something or running from something.

"Meet me out by the barn," Daisy told her.

Daisy waited for Blanche to slip out the door, and a few minutes later, she joined her outside. The women paid no heed when she disappeared. Only Mary and Daisy had become her friends. The others were merely acquaintances.

Daisy opened the barn door and the two slipped inside. "You know what happened to me, right."

"Yes," Blanche said. "My papa said I would never have a season for that very reason. Too many scalawags."

Not that they really had the money or even the clothes for her to wear. Her one nice dress was old and Mrs. Newton had tossed it, saying it was out of fashion. Whatever that meant.

"He was right," Daisy told her. "I need your help. Tonight, late, I want to sneak out and hang this sign on Thomas's gate, so that everyone will see it in the morning."

Blanche glanced at the sign and laughed. It was perfect to get Daisy's message across. "Oh, this sounds like what I've been missing. I've felt so stifled sitting around in that house all day just waiting for the time for us to leave. I'm sick of it. Needlepoint bores me and the women are so depressing. Wish I didn't have to leave."

The thought of Rusty brought tears to her eyes.

While she knew she had no reason to stay – there was nothing for her here – this was her home. And she was about to go someplace far away where she knew no one. It was a huge risk. A guaranteed new start or a complete failure. She couldn't take many more failures. She just couldn't.

"Agreed. What do you think of my sign?"

Blanche smiled and read out loud. 'Beware Defiler Rapist. Guard Your Daughters.' Perfect."

"I'm so excited. We'll need to slip out around midnight, sneak through the streets, and then put this on his gate. We can't get caught."

Yes, she was taking a huge risk, but she needed some excitement. Blanche had gotten a small amount of revenge and Daisy needed to get hers.

"I'll meet you out here at midnight," Blanche told her. "I'm so excited we're doing this."

Later, at the stroke of midnight, Blanche stood waiting for Daisy out by the barn. She'd dressed in her old men's clothing that she refused to let Mrs. Newton throw out. It felt good to have her familiar clothes on. But it also brought back memories.

The girl in these clothes could no longer exist. Now she must become a lady in order to get what she wanted.

"You look great," Daisy told her. "If I had some men's clothing I would have done the same."

"Sorry, I only saved the one set. I'm hoping once I get settled, I can wear them again."

Though that would depend on if her husband would accept her wearing pants.

"Let's get this done and get back. We're leaving early in the morning," Daisy said.

Blanche was so glad to finally be getting on the train out of town.

"Let's go," Blanche said, picking up the sign. "Grab some more wire. Let's make this difficult for him to remove."

"I like your way of thinking," Daisy told her, grabbing the small spool of bendable wire.

They opened the barn door glanced out and then took the back alleys to the mansion that sat on a small rise in the middle of town. They were quiet as they snuck along the shadowy passages and streets to reach the home they were searching for. Once, they heard voices and hid in the shrubbery until two drunks went stumbling by.

"Geez, it's past midnight. Don't they know they should be home?" Daisy whispered.

They reached the gate and stood there for a moment watching to make certain Jones didn't have guards or someone watching the house. No one. It was silent.

Quickly they began to work on hanging the crudely made sign on the gate. They wrapped wire around the iron rods so it would take a while to get down.

When they finished, they stood back and admired their handiwork. Giggling quietly, they ran down the street toward the alleys that would lead them back to Mrs. Newton's home.

When they reached the house, they snuck back inside. Daisy hugged Blanche.

"Thank you. That meant a lot to me."

"You're welcome. That was the most fun I've had in two weeks. Now we better get in bed. We have a long day tomorrow."

A day that would be so difficult. So hard to leave, once and for all, everything behind.

Quietly they went to their separate bedrooms to await the morning sun.

Early the next morning, Mrs. Newton had them all up, packed, fed, and out the door before the clock struck nine.

Today was the day.

Some of the girls were excited, but Blanche felt torn. She was leaving the only place she knew. Her father was buried here. Her birthright was here. And Rusty. All week long, she'd wanted to sneak out and go see her beloved dog, but knew leaving him a second time would be heartrending.

She couldn't do it. And it wouldn't be good for him to see her walk away from him a second time. Oh, how she missed his sweet kisses, his head bumping her leg begging for attention. The way he snuggled with her at night.

Mrs. Newton stood in front of the ticket counter at the train station, giving each girl a hug and handing out tickets.

This was it. They were leaving. Her final moments in Charleston.

A tear trickled down her cheek.

"Stop crying, Blanche. You're going to do well. Always remember you're a lady."

"But I'm leaving everything behind," she said with a whimper.

"Think of your new beginning."

As much as she'd tried, that was hard to do. She had no idea what Montana looked like. What her husband would look like. What if no one chose her for a wife?

"Look to the future," Mrs. Newton said and gave her one final hug. "Now, off you go. Does everyone have their tickets?" Mrs. Newton asked the ladies.

Blanche held hers up.

"Now, girls, remember, you can come back to Charleston if this is not what you want. They will pay your way home."

There was nothing to return to.

Just then she saw the sheriff walking down the platform. Were they coming for her? Had her burning the barn caught up with her?

He stopped in front of Mrs. Newton and she pointed to Daisy and then she walked beside him.

"Daisy, the sheriff wants to talk to you."

Thank God, it wasn't Blanche. Turning, she walked onto the train to reach safety. No sense waiting around to see if they wanted to speak to her. She was going to quietly disappear onto the train.

The conductor took her ticket and showed her to her seat. Sitting there, she wondered if Daisy would be kept behind.

Then she saw her as she made her way toward her seat. When she passed by Blanche, she winked at her.

And the two women giggled, sharing a secret.

The train blew its whistle and Blanche glanced around at the women. They were all in the same area of the train but sitting on different benches. Three months they would be traveling before they reached their destination.

Alice was sitting across from her and Blanche sent her a smile. There was nothing protecting her now. One smart comment out of her pretty pink mouth and Blanche would make her pay.

As much as she wanted to be a lady, it was hard to forget how Alice had treated her as a child. And she would never accept her bullying as an adult.

Blanche filled her eyes with the city of her birth. The hours of playing chase with Rusty. The home she'd left behind. The land that was rightfully hers.

Damn her father for his gambling ways.

God, how she wanted to stay but knew that was not possible.

"To new beginnings," Daisy said quietly.

"To new beginnings," Mary replied.

"To new beginnings," Blanche said.

The train whistle blew and the engine began to move toward her destiny. Toward her new husband and Montana.

CHAPTER 5

*M*artin Sanders sat by the glowing campfire staring deeply into the flames. The last few days he and Jakob had been working the cattle up in the high country. It was peaceful here and he liked they were away from the house, camping outside and experiencing the beautiful country they lived in, the land his family helped settle.

Here he felt free. Here he felt one with the earth. It seemed to be the only place he was at peace.

"The women are due in next week," Jakob said. "We need to decide if we're going to take a bride or not."

Martin tossed a stick into the flames. He had no desire to marry or have a wife and raise children. In fact, he struggled to get from one day to the next. Why add anyone else to this picture?

He didn't deserve love.

He would never leave Montana unlike his partner Jakob.

"You still thinking about leaving Montana?" Martin asked, knowing they were idiots for even considering a wife if Jakob planned on returning to South Carolina.

If Jakob left, he could not be responsible for a family.

Jakob sat across from him and shrugged. "I'm tired of sleeping with whores. I want a proper wife. Someone who is all sweet and innocent. Someone who will be the kind of wife I can be proud of. A lady, through and through."

In Martin's eyes, the man had an unrealistic vision of a wife. Sure, Martin wanted a woman who they would be proud to call wife, but he wasn't certain any woman could be what Jakob expected.

And Martin knew he could not be trusted to keep her safe. Or any children they might have.

"If we don't marry someone next spring, I'll be leaving for South Carolina."

Damn, the man was resorting to blackmail. If he didn't get his way, he was going.

They were best friends, better than brothers, and Martin didn't want him to leave. Call him selfish, but Jakob kept him sane. He'd been the one to convince him to stop working in the mine. To suggest they buy enough land and start a ranch. He'd been the one who talked him out of killing himself.

And now he was thinking of walking out of his life.

"If we marry a woman, what would happen if you decided to leave? Would I be the one she would stay with? Or would you take her back to South Carolina?"

There was silence. "Don't know. I guess that would be up to her to decide."

And Martin could not take care of her.

"Why are we even considering this if you're talking of leaving? Maybe you should decide what you want before we marry a woman."

In the darkness, Martin heard a coyote howl in the distance. The night sky was filled with stars, the moon a sliver.

"Because it's the only reason for me to stay," he said. "The ranch is doing well. You could continue it and just send me money. I need something more, Martin. I'm hoping a wife will fill this need. I feel restless. Someday I want children."

What if a woman didn't fill his need? Martin would be taking care of everything while Jakob ran off to get into trouble again in South Carolina.

"I understand you want to see your family. But we would be your new family," Martin said, fearing that Jakob would leave him with a wife and kids. And he had to decide if that was what he wanted. "The reason women share a husband here in Treasure Falls is because so many men die in the mine. You want us to marry and then you just leave when you're ready? That's not fair to me or the woman."

What if Martin died? Who would take care of their family then? What if he did the unthinkable? Somedays the guilt overcame him, and it was all he could do to face the day. Somedays even waking up seemed more than he could handle.

The fire popped, the sparks exploding in the air, sending a shower up into the darkness.

Sometimes Jakob could be selfish. And yet Martin knew that Jakob would take a bullet for him. Jakob would protect him. Jakob could make Martin see reason when the shame overcame him and he just wanted to end it all.

"If we marry and I'm happy, then I'll stay. But she must be more like my mother and sisters. She has to be a proper young woman, not a whore. Besides, I thought you were feeling better."

There were days when he would only remember that day once or twice during the daylight, but there were also days when the sounds of the walls collapsing closed in on him, the dust choking him, and he remembered running and screaming for everyone to get out. Get out now.

Only, so many didn't make it out. And at night, his dreams were filled with the screams of the miners.

"I have my days. But I don't want to bring a woman into our lives if you're not going to be here. She shouldn't be left with just me to take care of her."

There was silence around the fire and he could see that Jakob was carefully considering his words.

"You need to get over this. Maybe a woman could help you see that it wasn't your fault."

If that was possible, he would have found a woman long ago, but it was his fault. He hadn't done enough. He should have done more.

"I'm not getting married if I don't think I can protect a woman again. I'm not getting married if I think you're going to leave. Make your mind up on what you want to do. You can't leave me with a woman and children to take care of."

There was more silence.

The fire was beginning to die down and Martin threw another log on. Life had been carefree until the accident. Now, he lived with the pain every day. Now, he lived in the shadow of the man he once was. Now, he lived with the screams and the sounds of rocks sliding and crashing, killing everyone in their way.

"How about if we compromise. Let's check out the women and see if there is anyone we're interested in. Then if we find someone, we'll make a decision about what to do next. After all, I'm going to be very picky and this may all be for nothing. These eight women could be as homely as an old maid."

It was true. They might not be worth considering.

"So you're going to stay?"

"I'm not making any promises. I'm saying let's see what kind of women arrive. If we find a prim-and-proper woman, I could change my mind."

Just like Jakob. He always left himself an opening and a way to get out of making a promise. But if it would keep him in Treasure Falls, Martin really didn't have a choice.

"All right. Let's finish here tomorrow and head back to the ranch. Next week, we'll see the women and then we'll decide whether or not to make a union with one of them."

"Get some sleep, Martin," Jakob said, lying back on his pallet. "And for God's sake, get over feeling so guilty. I'm telling you, there was nothing any of us could have done."

"Easier said than done," he muttered.

A wife. They were going to look at the women coming

in to find themselves a proper wife. Why did he feel like once again Jakob had gotten his way?

CHAPTER 6

They were getting close. For two nights, the women on the stage had slept along the trail with the drivers keeping watch. Each night, the sound of the coyotes had sung them to sleep.

Blanche had loved every moment except the night she'd been ill. Food poisoning. And she suspected Alice Burns had fed her some old food, hoping she'd die along the way.

Why the woman hated her, she didn't understand. But she had bullied her since she was a child.

The woman said she was a good, Christian woman, but Blanche had her doubts. If anyone was going to start trouble, it was Alice. So far, Blanche had not decked Alice, but she'd better watch her back.

The food poisoning was close to the last straw for Blanche. Tossing her last meal beneath the stars was not fun. She'd been miserable.

Daisy sat up with her, feeding her hot tea and crackers.

Holding her hand when she threw up and making certain she was not alone. She considered her a real friend.

Her first.

In the distance, the mountains rose and touched the heavens. Snow clung to their tops and it was a sight Blanche had never seen. Beautiful and majestic, strong and powerful. Just like she was doing her best to become.

The air was cooler, and sometimes at night, she grew cold and frigid, pulling her blankets closer to the fire. After being sick, she felt vulnerable.

Especially when she suspected someone in their party had made her ill.

Thankfully, today they would reach their destination and she would no longer be near Alice or, at least, she hoped she wouldn't.

Since they left this morning, fear rode her the way she rode a horse, wild and free. Would a man choose her for his wife? What would he look like? Would he have the ranch she wanted?

So many questions, and if she was disappointed, she would have given up everything for nothing.

Looking out the window, she realized the last few days of the trip had been the most grueling and she was ready to get out of the box on wheels. Ready to begin her new life.

Today was the last stop before her future would be decided. The stage came to a halt and she realized they were being given a break. Suddenly the stagecoach driver opened the door.

"Ladies, we're taking a ten-minute break."

Blanche stepped out of the stage and stretched. Riding

in that rattletrap was a killer. She'd bounced all over that hard seat and even hit her head a time or two.

"You recovered," Alice said, walking up and smiling at her. The sneer on the woman's face sent her over the edge.

Without thinking, she drew back her fists and popped her in the nose. "You poisoned me, you witch, and now you're gloating about it? I could have died."

There was a gasp as the women watched them.

Daisy stepped between them. "Now, ladies. We've made it this far, let's not fight."

"I didn't poison you," Alice said, tears welling in her eyes. "I could never hurt someone. You punched me. You're vile and evil and nothing but white trash. If I'd poisoned you, you would be dead."

Blanche stepped forward to hit her again and Daisy grabbed her hand.

"Alice, unless you want to greet your husband with a black eye, I suggest you walk away. Enough."

The woman smiled a smirky smile at her, wiped her fake tears away, and strolled off. "White trash."

Daisy turned to Blanche. "Ignore her. Today is the end of the journey. We have so much to be thankful and happy about. You can't go around hitting people with your fists."

Blanche clenched her hands together, so badly wanting to hit the woman again.

"You know how bad I felt after she fixed my dinner."

Daisy's eyes pleaded with her, and she knew her friend was doing her best to help her. "I know, but you're letting her spoil this special day. Walk away from her."

"Just like you walked away from Thomas?"

Daisy frowned. "I'd have done more if I could have."

"Exactly. She needs to stay away from me or I'm going to pummel her good."

A sigh escaped from her friend. "And what will your husband think?"

"I don't care," she said, realizing she was not acting like a lady. With a growl, she shook her head. "All right. I'll remember I'm a lady. But Alice needs to stay away from me."

Laughter came from Daisy as she took her by the arm. They walked around the area stretching their legs.

The stagecoach driver came out of the bushes and glanced at them.

"Ladies, this is your last stop before we reach Treasure Falls. We'll be arriving within the hour. Get on board," their driver said.

"Just a moment," Francis Wiles said. It was rumored that she worked in a saloon in charge of the dice table.

The women all gathered around and Francis pulled out some dice. "Let's throw to see who gets off the stage first."

The women threw the dice and Daisy came in second with Blanche third.

"That's not fair," Alice whined and it was all Blanche could do not to knock her out. But that wouldn't be lady-like. She had to remember to act like a lady, not a hooligan.

"You're so right, Alice. Life can be very unfair at times," Blanche said, trying to use the same type of tone and words that she thought Mrs. Newton would have said.

"Bitch," Alice said beneath her breath.

Blanche pasted a fake smile on her face and ignored the

woman. It would not do to arrive in Treasure Falls with a bruised cheek or bloody hands from fighting. She had to remember to always act like a lady.

Though she did not feel like one. And doubted she ever would.

"That's it. Let's go," the driver said as they all began to climb back in the wooden contraption.

"Last time. I don't think I ever want to ride in a stage-coach again," Mary said.

"Me too," Blanche replied.

When the stage started up, the women had grown quiet as they bounced around on their way to meet their husbands.

Blanche had never dreamed of a big wedding. She'd never had a suitor or anyone who sought her pleasure. But she had dreamed of a family. And no matter what, she would never leave her children. Nothing could take her from them.

She would be a good mother, unlike her own mother.

The horses picked up speed and the women glanced at one another knowing that soon, they would be arriving.

Soon they would face their destiny. Soon they would meet their husbands.

CHAPTER 7

Martin and Jakob stood with all the other single men on the street waiting for the stage. They had been waiting about half an hour and expected it any time.

Aunt Grace glanced at the watch pinned to her dress. "The stage normally arrives at two p.m., but it could be late today."

A grumble rumbled amongst the men. Though it was Saturday, most of them worked six days a week in the mine. Today, the mine had let everyone off. The owner, Martin's brother, stood at the front of the group, waiting as well.

The Sanders family owned most of the town's stores. But they were good and fair people, and Jakob really liked them. He just wished that Martin's parents had lived longer.

Martin stood off to the side, his arms crossed, his hat pulled down over his face. The man wasn't mingling amongst the other men and talking. He stood off by himself almost like he was asleep, but Jakob knew better.

This was his attempt to show disinterest. They would be lucky to have a woman interested in them if this was how he acted.

The woman was not for Jakob so much as she was for Martin. The man needed the comfort of a woman's arms. Several years ago, life had dealt him a serious blow. One that he had yet to get over. And there was nothing he could have done to prevent the accident. Nothing.

But he refused to see that he was not to blame.

Jakob had been there; he'd witnessed the event and gone in search of Martin. Another five minutes deeper in the mine and he would not have gotten out alive. No one in the depths of the mine survived.

He gazed around at the men waiting. It was a strange group. Some miners, the banker, the mercantile owner, the mine owner, several ranchers, and even the blacksmith in town. So many single men.

Did they even have a chance of finding a wife?

He glanced around at the small town of Treasure Falls and knew he enjoyed living here. It was so different from living in Charleston. He wondered if he would know any of the women getting off the stage.

That would be strange if he knew one of them.

Doubtful. He hadn't been home in almost eight years. And when he'd left, his name was not one most people wanted anything to do with. Yet the urge to return home and see his family was strong.

He missed them.

The desire to ride back into town a wealthy man, the prodigal son returning, rode him hard. But it was clear across the country and how would the people accept him? After all, he'd fought a duel with the son of a wealthy man in town. Thank goodness he'd not killed him, but dueling was outlawed. And the law came looking for him.

A hot-headed teenager, he thought he was protecting a his sister's reputation. Only after the duel, his mother kicked him out.

At this point, he was even tired of the whores who took his money, did the deed, and then pointed to the door. So cold and classless.

No, his wife would have to be the perfect example of comportment. A true lady, through and through, who obeyed her husband and was an example to their children.

"Stage is coming," someone shouted.

Aunt Grace jumped up and down. "The women are arriving. Get ready men. Be on your best behavior and don't act forward. Anyone who does will have to answer to me."

He laughed. The woman was tough and she didn't mess around. He'd seen her throw a man out of her home because he'd been rude. No one messed with Aunt Grace.

The stage came around the corner.

"Men, line up, the women will walk down and you'll get a chance to meet all of them. Remember first impressions are very important."

There were two stages arriving and some of the women were hanging out the window. A beautiful auburn hair woman sat at the window, gazing out at the men. She leaned forward a little and he almost groaned. She was gorgeous. All that silken auburn air flowing down past her shoulders.

But was she a lady?

Martin walked up beside him.

"Best behavior, Martin," he said.

"I heard," the man replied. "The question is whether or not we're going to find a woman you'll consider."

A grin spread across his face. While Martin thought he was doing this for him, it was really for Martin. The man needed a wife. He needed a woman to help comfort him and ease his pain.

"Do you see anyone you're interested in?" Jakob asked, his eye on the auburn-haired woman.

Martin half laughed. "Hell, it's been so long since I've been with a woman, any of them look mighty nice. But that red-haired woman. Damn, she's beautiful."

Jakob felt his heart slam into his chest. Maybe this was going to work out after all. Maybe he could find a wife that Martin was attracted to and met his own criteria, and then he would have no reason to go home.

His home would be here.

"I think you've got fine taste. Let's just hope she's prim and proper. With all that red hair, her spirit could be just as fiery."

A deep-throated chuckle came from Martin. "If she's fiery in the bedroom, that would make it even better."

Jakob's cock hardened at the thought of spreading her across the bed and taking her.

"But first, we have to court her," Jakob replied. "First we have to learn if she's a good woman."

The men were yelling and waving their hats.

"First, we have to see if she's even interested in a couple of cowboys like us," Martin said.

The stage pulled to a stop, and after the driver set the brake, he stepped down and opened the door.

The first two women were beautiful, but Jakob felt his heart slam into his chest when the red-haired woman alighted from the stage.

"Damn," he said beneath his breath. "If she's not the one, I'll be damned."

"I'm with you," Martin said. "Those curves and all that red hair are enough to knock me off my feet. Let's just hope she has a sweet personality to go with her looks."

"A demure and ladylike personality."

CHAPTER 8

*B*lanche felt like she was suffocating. The anxiety of what she would face when they arrived was beginning to get to her. She leaned her head out the window just as the stage rolled into town.

A quaint little town came into view. A bank, a mercantile, a restaurant, and a saloon, with a couple of other unnamed buildings were on Main Street.

No hotel. Where would they stay? Or would they marry a man upon arrival? She knew what she wanted. She wanted a rancher. She didn't want to live in town. She refused.

She wanted the life she'd lost.

The largest house had a sign out front. Dr. Owen Sanders.

"No hotel? Where will we stay?" Daisy asked.

"I don't know. Look, there is a group of people standing in front of a building. Oh, dear, it's the men," Mary said.

Blanche saw a group of handsome young men standing

out front and realized this was it. This was the beginning of their new life.

Unable to look away, Blanche continued to hang out the window, unease filling her. What if she didn't find what she was looking for? What would she do then?

Somehow she had to believe she would find what she was searching for. A rancher. A man with land and cattle and horses.

"We'll always be friends," Daisy said, tears filling her eyes.

"Yes, always. No matter what happens," Mary said.

The stagecoach driver pulled on the reins and the horses slowed and the coach came to a stop.

Blanche pulled back from the window. She felt like she was going to be sick again. That damn Alice had done this to make her look bad, but she was not going to let illness overcome her.

"This is it," Mary said.

A roar from the men outside filled the air.

"Oh, look how handsome they all are," Blanche said. "We're getting married."

The door suddenly opened. "Ladies, you have arrived."

Nausea gripped Blanche. At the last stop, they had thrown dice to see who would alight first and in what order. Mary had won the draw and Daisy was second. Blanche would be third and Rose would be right behind her.

This was it.

Swallowing the fear and nausea, she watched as Mary

took the driver's hand and stepped from the stage. Then it was Daisy's turn.

"Good luck."

"You too," they said.

Blanche watched her friend greeting the men and then the stagecoach driver was waiting for her. It was her turn to step from the coach.

"Take a deep breath and smile. You're beautiful. Any man out there would be lucky to have you for his bride," Rose said.

Her heart seemed to melt at the woman's words.

"Thank you," she said. "I needed to hear that."

"Go get 'em," she said with a smile.

Stepping out of the coach, Blanche stopped and took a deep breath before she walked up to the waiting group of men.

Plastering a smile on her face, she shook hands with the first four men and then she reached a man who smiled at her shyly, his big brown eyes filled with wonder. Dark lashes lay on his high cheekbones and the way his lips turned up to greet her had her tilting her head.

There was something about him that seemed to draw her.

"Blanche Underwood," she said.

"Martin Sanders of the Lucky Strike Ranch," he said, pushing his off-white cowboy hat back from his face.

The man looked like a rancher with his arms all muscled up, his shirt fit him tightly across his chest, and she wondered how it would feel to lay her head there.

"Did you say ranch?" she said, gazing at him, hoping he was really a rancher.

"Yes," he replied. "We own about one hundred acres just outside of town."

"I'm a ranching girl," she said. "My family owned fifty acres of some of the best grassland in South Carolina. We raised cattle and horses and even had a couple hundred sheep."

He grinned at her. "Welcome to Treasure Falls."

"Thank you," she said, hoping she hadn't made a complete fool of herself, but knowing she wanted to live on a ranch. It was where she belonged.

She stepped to the next man.

"Blanche Underwood."

"Jakob Moore. Martin and I own the Lucky Strike together."

She nodded, not wanting to seem obsessed with their ranch. His large blue eyes seemed to twinkle at her.

This man was just as handsome as the previous one. Why had these men not found wives?

He wore a brown cowboy hat that he pushed back as he stared at her like he'd just received a Christmas present.

"You're a redhead," he said.

"Yes, I am," she said. "My mother was full Irish and had red hair."

The way he gazed at her made her feel kind of breathless and hot. She had two men she wanted to know more about.

"I've always had a thing for redheads."

She grinned at him. The man's smile sent a little tingle down her spine. Both of these men were exactly what she was looking for as long as they were nice. But she needed to know more about them. If one was a gambler, he was out.

"Save a seat for us at your table tonight," Jakob said.

She moved farther down and suddenly a woman was standing in front of her.

"Sorry, I had to get out of line. Welcome, I'm Grace Sanders. You'll be staying in our home until you marry," she said smiling. "We're so excited to have you ladies. Welcome to Treasure Falls."

"Thank you," Blanche said. She'd forgotten all about where they were going to stay the night. She'd been too concentrated on finding herself a rancher to marry.

As she walked down the line of men, she couldn't help but glance back at Martin and Jakob. There was something about them that drew her, and no, it wasn't just the fact they owned a ranch.

Though that was a delicious perk.

She made it through the rest of the men and caught up with Daisy.

"What do you think?"

"I think we're some very lucky women," Daisy said softly.

Blanche smiled. She thought so too.

When everyone was off the stage, a man named Jesse whistled loud enough to get everyone's attention.

"We're having a supper tonight at Uncle Owen's and Aunt Grace's home at six thirty. For now, we're going to let the ladies get settled in, clean the dust off, and rest before the evening's festivities."

Sitting on something that wasn't moving sounded like a splendid plan. That would also give her time to freshen up before she met the men for the second time today. This was it and a spurt of excitement went through her.

She hoped and prayed she had not left everything behind for nothing.

The aunt smiled at everyone. "We have a pig roasting and our cook is making lots of good food for tonight. You are to dress in clean attire to meet these ladies. And, of course, we will expect everyone to be on their very best behavior."

Aunt Grace walked to the front of the line. "Follow me, ladies."

As they walked down the street, she noticed all the small shops. Compared to Charleston, Treasure Falls was not even a tenth of the size. It was such a small, pretty town.

Blanche wanted to turn around and gaze one last time at Martin, but didn't want to appear easy, so she just kept walking. If her man wasn't Martin, maybe it would be Jakob.

Both were two very fine choices. Both were part owners of the Lucky Strike Ranch.

CHAPTER 9

*L*ater that evening when Aunt Grace called her name, Blanche made her way down the stairs. She'd worn her best gown, a purple dress that made her auburn hair glow and her emerald eyes shine.

Mrs. Newton had picked the dress out just for her and she felt honored to wear the beautiful gown.

Nervous, she looked around and saw Jakob and Martin, the two men she'd met earlier this evening. They met her at the bottom of the stairs and she smiled at them.

"Hello," she said. "It's good to see you again."

When she reached the floor, the doctor came over and escorted her to stand by Daisy. Then the other girls came down the stairs until they all were in the same room.

The doctor stood between the men and women.

"Welcome, ladies, we're so glad you're here. Tonight is a chance for all of you to get to know one another. The men will tell you who their partner is so you'll get to know both of the men at once. You have two weeks to make up your mind before we will have a wedding ceremony right here in the house. You'll marry one man and the other will be your second husband."

Blanche shook her head. Did he just say they would have two husbands? She glanced at Daisy and then Mary who was standing board straight. The women appeared stunned. So Blanche had not imagined she'd heard him say *two husbands*.

"Excuse me," Rose Patton said. "What are you talking about two husbands?"

There was chattering among the women.

The doctor appeared a little shaken.

"In Treasure Falls, there are two husbands for each woman. We have lived this way for many years, due to the shortage of women. This way if one husband is killed, the second man is there to make certain the family is taken care of."

Hysterical laughter bubbled up within Blanche. Not one man, but two.

Two husbands…

The noise in the room seemed to explode with the women turning to one another and asking if they had been told there would be two husbands.

"Quiet please," the doctor said.

"I'm sorry, but we were not told this," Mary said. "We thought we were coming to a place where there was one man for each woman."

What did you do that was different with two men? Being a rancher, she understood the physical act between a man and a woman, but two? How did that work?

Jesse walked up beside his uncle. "This has been our way since Treasure Falls began for many different reasons. It's not a bad way to live. You have a legal husband and also a second man who will love and take care of you."

The women were all gazing at one another, confusion reigning. Should they stay or return to Charleston?

Blanche wasn't going anywhere. And in some ways, this made her decision so much easier. Now she didn't have to choose between Martin and Jakob. Now she could have both of them. And that felt kind of lucky.

"Ladies, I've lived this way all my life and my husbands have kept me very happy. Sadly, Silas died last year. So, now, it's just me and the doctor," Aunt Grace said.

Blanche glanced at Martin and Jakob and smiled. She wanted them to know she was all right with having two husbands. She would sleep with Martin one night, and then the next, she'd sleep with Jakob. This wasn't a problem at all.

The tension in the room seemed to stifle the party atmosphere that had existed a few moments ago.

"Did the matchmaker not mention this?" Jesse asked.

"No," Mary said. "I'd like to know more about this way of life. I'd like to talk to Grace in private sometime. We have two weeks before we have to make a decision. I'm willing to consider having two husbands."

"Me too," Daisy said.

"I will as well," Blanche said, looking around to find Martin and Jakob. Jakob winked at her, and a spiral of heat scampered down her spine.

Slowly, the women agreed to learn more, and once

again, the atmosphere changed. The atmosphere became happier, and only Alice Burns and Rose Patton seemed upset by the news.

"Well, then, ladies and gentlemen, let's mingle and get to know one another," the doctor said smiling.

He moved out of the way just in time as the men came rushing toward the women. Martin and Jakob appeared at her side.

Each man took her elbow.

"That dress is stunning on you," Martin said as he took hold of her arm. His dark brown eyes were beautiful and staring at her; it almost took her breath away. His nose was straight and his cheekbones were high and defined like he'd been chiseled from granite.

And those full lips had her wondering how his kiss would be. She'd never been kissed. Never. And she was determined that before the night was over, she was going to experience some man's lips.

Hopefully, it would be Martin's.

"Thank you," she said, loving the feel of his fingers on her skin. Warmth spread through her arm.

"Now, I understand why the two of you were together today," she said, smiling at them, wondering what it would feel like to be sandwiched between two strong, husky men.

She'd never experienced one man, and if they chose her, she would have two men showing her the ways between a man and a woman.

Maybe she was wrong, but she had to make certain before she committed to anyone that she wasn't marrying a gambler. That would send her running in the opposite direction.

"Let's go sit outside while they get the dinner ready," Jakob said.

She could feel him watching her. His sharp blue eyes were gazing at her, and she could see he was determining what kind of woman she was. Well, wouldn't he be surprised? Her lessons had paid off, and she was a lady.

Martin opened the door and they both waited while she glided through just like Mrs. Newton showed her. When she stepped outside onto a patio area, there were gas lanterns hanging throughout the area making it feel cozy. Small tables were scattered about so everyone could sit and chat without others nearby.

With a glance, she saw that Mary and Daisy were sitting outside talking to some men.

Jakob pulled out her chair and she sank down.

They took chairs on either side of her.

"What made you decide to come to Montana?" Martin asked, gazing at her.

The man had the sweetest mouth and his eyes were kind. And yet, an air of sadness seemed to pervade him.

"Great question," she said. "My father, who is now deceased, was a gambler. We had fifty acres of some of the best farmland near Charleston. He lost it in a poker game."

The anger of losing the land that day came back, but she successfully held it back, remembering that she was a lady, and ladies didn't show their emotions.

"I had to move out of my childhood home. Leave

behind family heirlooms, but most of all my dog. He didn't deserve to be forced into another home in his old age."

The pain of leaving him still stung.

"How did you meet the matchmaker?" Jakob asked.

"Mrs. Newton was putting up flyers advertising for mail-order brides. I spoke to her and she told me to move in with her until the train left. Here I am."

Jakob frowned at her, his emerald eyes darkening in the lantern light that was above them. "What about your mother?"

"My mother ran off with the pan salesman when I was five. I never saw her again," she said.

Martin reached out and took her hand. "So you've never had a woman's touch."

"No, my father raised me," she said, remembering not to say *papa*. "And if either one of you gambles, please tell me now. That is a complete deal breaker for me. In fact, why did you name your ranch the Lucky Strike?"

Jakob leaned back in his chair, his eyes carefully assessing her. "Martin named the ranch the Lucky Strike because he used to work in the mine. Most of his family's money comes from the mine, or it did before his brother bought it."

"Oh," she said, thanking God the money wasn't from gambling. "But you didn't answer my question. Do either one of you gamble?"

"I have in the past," Martin said. "But not here. There is no gambling hall here. We have a saloon, but no gambling is allowed. I've never been good at winning money, so I don't enjoy it."

She nodded and turned to Jakob.

"No, I don't gamble. I'm not about to lose my hard-earned money."

While she knew they could be lying to her, she felt like they were being honest. "Good. After losing our ranch, I want nothing to do with someone who gambles."

They sat there for a moment. Martin ran his thumb over her hand. It was a soothing feeling that had her breathing funny.

"What about the two of you? Are your families here?"

Martin glanced at Jakob and she could tell he was sending him some kind of message.

"My parents are both dead," he said. "But I have six brothers and a sister."

"Oh my, that's a large family."

"Yes, it is," Martin said. "And so far, we all live here. It's hard to get together, but you'll meet several of them tonight."

"Oh," she said, glancing around.

"My mother and three sisters all live back in Charleston, of all places," Jakob said. She could feel him scrutinizing her. "Have you heard of Sarah Moore?"

The Moore family was a big society family and she'd never come into contact with them because they didn't have anything to do with ranchers like her father and herself.

"No, I'm sorry, I haven't," she said. She wondered if he would check up on her. Well, she had told him the truth about herself. She had nothing to hide. Her family would never have been considered on the same social level as his was. She and her papa were poor ranchers.

Just then the cook announced the food was ready.

"I'll get your plate for you," Jakob told her.

"Thank you," she said.

"Martin, you stay with Blanche."

A smile crossed his face and he stared at her. "You're just so pretty. What other questions do you have for us?"

"How many horses do you have? Tell me about your ranch," she said.

The man's eyes rose. "You really are a rancher."

"Oh, yes, I loved working with the animals," she said, not wanting to hide what made her happy. "It was so hard to leave them all behind. Especially my dog, Rusty."

Tears welled in her eyes and one trickled down her cheek. "Don't cry," Martin said softly.

"I'm sorry. He was such a loving dog and it broke my heart to leave him. I'd had him for over twelve years."

He reached over and thumbed the tear from her face. "I love dogs."

"Me too," she said. "We also had twenty horses a couple hundred cattle and twelve of the meanest goats."

Laughter bubbled up from him. "I hate goats. When Jakob and I started the ranch, I said no goats."

"The babies are sweet, but then they grow up to be mean little buggers."

For a moment, they just stared at one another before he lifted her hand to his lips. "I'll be honest and tell you, I wasn't certain I wanted a wife. You've made me reconsider. Having you as a wife would be good, just keep in mind that sometimes I can be difficult. Jakob, he wants a lady to be our wife. And you seem like you're very much a lady."

She started to laugh. "I try very hard to be a lady, but just like you, sometimes it can be difficult."

"Then I think you're going to be a perfect match for us," he said. "We have two weeks to get to know each other, but I can see no reason why you're not the one."

"Good," she said. "I'm very excited about living on a ranch again. But more than anything, I'm excited that I've found two men to be my husbands. You seem like the perfect match for me."

Without thinking, she reached over and pulled his mouth to hers. It was a soft, gentle kiss. A brief meeting of lips that she initiated because she'd never been kissed, and she wanted to experience how it felt.

Their lips barely touched and yet warmth filled her. When they moved apart, she smiled at him. "I'm sorry I was being forward. I've never been kissed before and I wanted to experience what it would feel like."

Shaking his head, he leaned toward her. "Oh, darling, that was not a real kiss. When we're not surrounded by people, I'll show you a real kiss. One that will make you melt in my arms."

The thought of a kiss being more was something she couldn't understand. So she leaned in closer to him.

"I can't wait."

CHAPTER 10

"*What* did you think of Blanche?" Martin asked Jakob as they rode along the road, the stars and moon lighting their way. Normally, they were not out this late, but tonight was an exception.

After a long day of being in town, Martin was ready to go home. And yet it had been more fun than he expected. He hadn't gone there today with the expectation of finding a wife. That just seemed impossible. Yet Martin knew he wanted to marry Blanche. And soon.

Talking to her tonight, he'd quickly realized she was everything he wanted in a woman. And he couldn't wait to slip his hand beneath her skirts. The simple kiss they'd shared had only made him eager for more. And he loved the way she'd been the one to initiate the simple tasting.

Blanche was a woman who went after what she wanted and it seemed like she wanted them.

It was obvious she'd never kissed a man before, but he liked her forwardness. He liked the way she went after what she wanted. He wondered how Jakob would feel if he knew they shared a kiss.

Maybe it was better if he didn't tell him. Because that's not how a proper young woman, a lady, as Jakob liked to say, acted. Martin couldn't care less if she was a lady. Of course, he wanted a good woman, but he wanted one who went after what she wanted.

Blanche seemed like that kind of girl.

"So far, I like what I see," Jakob said. "As long as she continues to act like a good woman, then I think we've found our wife."

The stars glistened in the night sky and a cool breeze blew.

Jakob was so possessed with finding a good woman. He had flaws. Martin had flaws, and any woman, regardless of who she was, would have flaws. No one could be good all the time.

Not even Jakob.

"I think your expectations are too much," Martin said. "Tell me what you expect of our wife."

There was silence as the horses moseyed along the trail that led to their ranch. The ride was peaceful as long as they didn't encounter a wolf or a bear.

"My mother dressed appropriately. She always looked nice like she was going to church. She did not curse or use swear words. I've never seen alcohol touch her lips, and she expected the men in her life to treat her like a respected woman. I never saw her run. She glided across the room much the way Blanche did tonight."

Unfortunately, everything he said was something good

about a woman. Maybe he should ask about what would cause him to break up with her.

"What would it take for you to decide that she's not the one?"

"That's easy. Smoking, cursing, drinking, fighting, going to a saloon. Anything that a true lady would never do."

Why he was so hung up on her being a lady, Martin didn't know. He liked her spirit.

"So if she wanted to work around the ranch, what would you think?"

"Never. She's our wife. Not a ranch hand."

Why did he get the feeling that Blanche had worked her ranch land? Why did he get the feeling she probably had no choice? And yet she appeared like a modest lady. She acted like what Jakob wanted, but somehow Martin felt there was more to her, and he was glad.

All that beautiful auburn hair had to mean something about her personality.

What Jakob wanted sounded boring. Really boring.

"I don't think she'd be too happy if we asked her to work the cattle," Jakob said.

"No, but she might like to go horseback riding," Martin replied.

"We should buy her a sidesaddle."

Why did Martin get the feeling she wouldn't want a sidesaddle? There was a stubborn streak that resided inside Blanche that he truly believed she was trying to hide, but eventually there would be no hiding her determination.

And a sidesaddle just didn't seem to fit her, and he was happy with that.

Eventually her true feelings and emotions would show, and he couldn't wait because he didn't want the woman that Jakob described. He wanted a real fire-and-ice kind of woman, who could be a lady to the world and a whore in the bedroom.

"What did you think of Blanche," Jakob said.

He thought long and hard about what he felt for the woman. She was beautiful and feisty and he could see her stubborn nature eager to escape. And yet he'd been smitten the moment he laid eyes on her.

"I'd marry her tomorrow," he said. "And I was the one who didn't want to marry a woman. There is something so intriguing about this girl that I can't wait to explore every inch of her."

He turned in the saddle and glanced at Jakob. The man stared at him in shock. Even in the darkness, he could see he was stunned.

"Amazing," he said finally. "I truly expected to return home tonight with no one in mind. And yet you're ready to say I do."

Martin didn't respond but continued riding toward the house at the end of the lane. Even if Jakob decided to return to South Carolina, at least he would have someone to keep him warm at night. In a short afternoon, he'd found the woman he wanted.

In a short afternoon, he'd changed his mind and decided he wanted love. He wanted Blanche.

But he worried about his nightmares. About the guilt

that ravaged him, and if Blanche would understand his pain. Would she accept that there were days he could barely get out of bed, let alone speak?

"There will be some trying times ahead, I'm certain of it," he said, thinking that most would be because of Jakob's expectations, and his own damn guilt that ate at him like a deadly disease. "But I truly believe she is our woman. Our wife. And I can't wait to spread her legs and drive my cock home deep."

Jakob laughed. "You're just eager to have a woman. It's been a while."

"I'm eager to spread a woman between us and for both of us to claim her together. And if you decide to leave, I'll miss you, but I'm all right with that now. I just hope that Blanche can understand why I feel bad some days."

They pulled up to the barn.

"Frankly, I hope she can help you realize that it wasn't your fault. You're not a murderer. Maybe she can help you see how many people you saved."

God, he wished he could see the disaster that way, but he didn't. All he could see were the dead bodies they carried out of the mine for days.

With a sigh, he threw his leg over the side of his horse. "No, I'm not a murderer, but a lot of people died because of me. And that's hard to live with."

CHAPTER 11

A week later, they drove into town to pick up Blanche and take her out to the falls. Tomorrow they planned to bring her to the ranch to see their place. Just about every other day, they did something together.

Slowly they were getting to know her, and so far, her lady persona had not cracked. She acted like a woman born to royalty.

The rest of the time was spent on their ranch making certain the cattle were fed and watered and the other assortment of animals were taken care of. Life on a ranch didn't let one walk away and play for two weeks.

And yet, Jakob was considering leaving and going to South Carolina to visit his family.

Time was flying by, and Jakob needed to be certain before he agreed to marry her. It was strange how Martin had come around and now was counting down the days before the ceremony.

The days before the wedding night.

The days before Blanche was theirs.

But Jakob still wasn't convinced she was the type of woman he wanted.

One moment, she was the perfect picture of a lady and he wanted to marry her, and then suddenly, she would do something and he would start to question whether Blanche was really who he could spend forever with.

Two weeks was not long to get to know someone, and yet, that was part of the contract. The women expected a marriage ceremony in two weeks.

Martin pulled the wagon up in front of Dr. Sanders's home.

Blanche came running down the stairs, dressed in a yellow dress and a straw hat perched on her head. The woman was gorgeous. But would a real lady run down the stairs?

Maybe she was eager to see them, but his mother always glided wherever she went.

Martin jumped out of the wagon and took her in his arms. Jakob sat back and watched the two. It was obvious that Martin was smitten with the girl, and even Blanche had a touch of pink on her cheeks as she gazed at him.

"Hello," she said. "I'm so happy to see you. What do you have planned for today?"

Slowly Jakob crawled out of the wagon and walked around to Blanche. He didn't want to appear over eager. It would be good for her to learn right now that he was the man in charge and he controlled how much affection she'd receive from him.

She would never receive all of his heart or his love, and she would have to adjust to that.

He kissed her on the cheek, though today, he planned on giving her the type of kiss that a lover gives his woman. How would she act when he tried to place his hands in places that he shouldn't?

This was a test. No self-respecting woman would allow a man to touch her. If she failed, the engagement would not happen.

In some ways, it felt mean to do this to her, and for that reason, he had not told Martin. The man would be angry with him and tell him he was being unkind. But Jakob had to test her.

How else would he know if she was a real lady? When she passed his test, then he would consider marrying her. But not until.

"Hello, Jakob," she said, giving him a teasing smile. "How are you today?"

"I'm good. You're looking very beautiful. We thought we would take you to the falls area and show you what the town was named for."

Taking his arm, she glanced up at him. "That sounds lovely. It's so good to be outdoors on this beautiful summer day."

Just then another woman came out the door and glared at Blanche. She stood at the top of the stairs, her hands on her hips, gazing at them.

Blanche turned and glanced up at her grinning.

"Bye, Alice, have a wonderful day," she said.

The woman's face turned into a grimace and Jakob

wondered why there seemed to be animosity between them.

"Let's go," she said. "I can't wait to spend the day with the two of you."

For some reason, Jakob felt that something was going on between the women, but Blanche didn't say anything and he didn't ask. It was none of his business.

Jakob walked her around the wagon and helped her up onto the bench seat. Martin climbed up beside her. They had her squeezed between them. Just like he hoped to someday have her in bed, right between them.

As the wagon began to roll, Blanche waved at the woman, smiling.

"Gentlemen, I want us to play a game when we get to the falls," she said.

Jakob frowned. He really wasn't into parlor games of any kind. "What kind of game."

"It's a surprise," she said, reaching out and grabbing his hand.

That was a little forward. He should be the one making the moves, not her.

"But I don't like games," he said, thinking he didn't want to play. He wanted to test her. See if she really was a lady.

The wagon rolled down the road and he watched as she grew excited. "Oh, look at the pine trees. They're so pretty. Does your ranch have pine trees?"

"No," Martin said. "There are some along the edges of the property, but we're in a valley that has lots of good grass for the cattle."

The wagon hit a rough spot in the road and it threw

Blanche up against Jakob. Not that he minded, but she didn't move quite as quickly as he would have liked.

Yet, the feel of her soft curves slamming into him almost had him groaning. The woman's full breasts and shapely hips were enough to have him dreaming of riding her, his cock slamming into her sweet, willing pussy.

Just then the wagon turned into the area near the falls.

"Listen to that. You can hear the water," she said, her big emerald eyes wide with amazement.

Martin pulled the wagon up beside the waterfalls in a grassy area. Jakob checked the surrounding area for animals. This was their watering hole and he didn't want to startle a mountain lion, a bear, or even a deer for that matter.

The wagon came to a halt.

"It's so beautiful," she said.

"There's a legend about the falls that you should know," Martin said, setting the brake and turning to her.

"An Indian warrior loved the chief's daughter. But the chief didn't think he was the right brave to marry her."

Jakob picked up the story. "The chief told the warrior if he could find the lost treasure of the Absaroka Range, he could marry his daughter. Thinking it was just an old fool's tale, the chief didn't believe in the treasure. And he didn't want his daughter marrying this warrior."

Martin jumped down out of the wagon and then reached back to help Blanche off, his hands around her slender waist.

Jakob wished his hands were touching her. For just a moment, he held her.

"The warrior loved the girl and searched for months for the treasure. Finally, he came back and told the chief that the treasure was in the falls near Helena," Martin said, his hand moving to the small of her back.

Jumping out of the wagon, Jakob took her hand and led Blanche to the water. Martin followed them.

"The old chief didn't believe he had found the treasure. Again, he refused to let the warrior marry his daughter. The couple felt they had waited long enough. Much to the chief's dismay and anger, they ran off together," Jakob said.

Martin gazed at the waterfall. "The old chief had the warriors in his tribe go after them. When they were about to be captured, the couple confessed their love for one another and dove into the falls together. They died in each other's arms."

Blanche gasped. "How sad."

Jakob smiled at her. "The legend says that you can sometimes see the faces of the Indian couple here or your dead loved ones. And that's the legend of Treasure Falls."

She pulled him toward the water. "Let's look. Maybe we'll see someone we know that's died. Or the couple. How neat it would be to see them so in love."

That was the problem. He didn't believe in the legend. It was just the story of someone's overactive imagination.

Jakob shook his head. "I don't believe in the legend. Maybe an Indian couple died here, but why would they hang around and show up to talk to people in this century?"

A frown drew her forehead together as she gazed at him with disappointment in her eyes.

"Maybe they want to help other lovers," she said softly, staring at him.

Laughing, Martin walked up beside Blanche. "Don't listen to him. I think it's a sweet story and people in town claim that they've seen loved ones here. Me, I don't want to see anyone."

Sadness filled his face and he walked away. He took a blanket out of the wagon and spread it on the ground.

Jakob knew Martin was thinking about his deceased parents and needed to get him out of this mood or he would sink into a dark place. A place that Jakob didn't want Blanche to see.

"Let's play your game," he said, pulling her back from the pond.

The falls continued to splash into the water, the spray making a rainbow over the waterfall.

"My game seems pale in comparison to the legend you told me."

When they reached the blanket, she sat just like a lady would, spreading her skirts about her. Maybe he was being paranoid. Maybe she truly was a lady.

"What kind of game is this?" Martin asked.

Jakob was relieved to see his friend had pulled himself out of the depths of his sadness.

"It's called Truth or Dare," she said. "I'm going to ask you which you prefer and then give you a question. I thought this would be a great way to get to know more about each other," she said grinning.

A cool breeze blew across the water, the spray settling on them. Blanche giggled and lifted her face to the wind. It was all Jakob could do not to pull her into his arms and run his tongue up her neck until he reached her lips and kiss her thoroughly.

That sweet mouth of hers was full and tempting, and he couldn't wait to taste her.

"Do we get to ask you questions?" Martin asked.

"Yes," she said. "And if you don't answer, you'll be punished."

"How?"

She thought for a moment.

"I know," Jakob said. "We'll pull you across our lap and spank you."

She shook her head. "No, that's not appropriate."

Martin laughed. "How about the person has to walk part way back to Treasure Falls."

"That would be bad," Blanche said. "I'm agreeable."

"You're not afraid of having to walk?"

"I have nothing to hide," she said smiling. "Who wants to go first?"

"I will," Martin said.

Just then another breeze blew and water droplets landed on them. Blanche licked the moisture off her lips with her tongue.

Jakob went rigid. Dear God, did she not realize what she was doing to him?

"Truth or dare?" she asked.

"Truth," Martin replied.

"Truth," Jakob said.

"What is the most embarrassing thing you've ever done?"

Martin started to laugh. "When I was twelve, I accidentally farted at the Christmas table. My mother was mortified. All the family had gathered, and her son farted."

Blanche smiled at him. Then she turned to Jakob. "What about you?"

"Most embarrassing thing? I hit a man with my fists and then later learned that he was innocent of the wrongdoing I had accused him of."

Blanche tilted her head and gazed at him. "But is that embarrassing?"

"I think so. I was wrong," he said. He'd gotten in so much trouble for hitting a man who was innocent. His mother had given him ten licks with the belt.

"All right, I'll take your answer."

"Who won that round?" Martin asked.

"No one. It's a tie," she said, gazing at them. "Truth or dare?"

"What happens if we take a dare?"

"Then I'll dare you to do something," she said.

"Maybe later," Jakob replied. He wanted to dare her and see how she would respond. This game could work into his plans perfectly.

"Truth," Martin said.

"Truth," Jakob replied.

"When has someone hurt you emotionally enough that you cried," she said.

"Not fair, men don't cry," Jakob said.

"Everyone cries," she replied. "You don't cry when you're hurting?"

"No," he said. "I don't allow people to hurt me."

"When my mother died, and a miner accused me of not telling the inspector about the crack in the wall."

Blanche was silent as she stared at Martin. She reached out and grabbed his hand and brought it up to her lips. "I'm so sorry. That had to hurt a lot."

Tears welled in Martin's eyes. "I've never hurt so bad. Still hurts to this day."

"I'm sure," she said as she pulled him to her and kissed him on the lips. It was a sweet innocent kiss and yet she'd instigated it. Ladies did not instigate kissing or touching or anything. That was a man's job.

And yet he couldn't help but think it was the right move. It was exactly what Martin needed.

But he was jealous. He wanted to kiss her. But he didn't want that kind of kiss. It was too sweet and innocent. No, he wanted one that would let her know exactly what she did to him. Let her feel his hard, rigid cock just waiting to take her.

There was a tense silence that fell between them.

"What about you, Jakob?"

"Probably when my mother kicked me out of the house," he said. He hadn't meant to tell her that. But after he'd gotten into a duel with a man who kissed his sister, he'd been expelled from the house and it was what sent him fleeing across the country away from the law.

"Did you go back?" she asked.

"One question at a time, but no. I came out to Montana and met Martin," he said, knowing there was so much more to the story, but not willing to share it just yet.

"Truth or Dare?"

"Truth," Martin said.

"Truth," Jakob said, wishing he could dare her, but wanting to wait and hear her answers before he made his move.

"I have one more question. What do you expect in a wife?"

"That doesn't seem to go with the other questions in the game," Jakob said.

"It doesn't, but I want to hear your answers," she said as she leaned back on her elbows and gazed at the two men.

Did the woman not realize that it was all he could do not to climb on top of her and let her feel exactly what he thought of her. His breath seemed to catch in his throat as he gazed at her and tried to concentrate on the game.

"I expect someone to love me for my good qualities and also my bad ones. I'm not a perfect human being. I've made some mistakes and will do so again. But I want a woman who is going to love me regardless," Martin said.

Blanche smiled at him. "I love your answer."

"Jakob?"

"I need a lady. A woman who is respectful and shows the town that I'm married to a genteel lady, who will be such an inspiration to my daughters and even my sons."

A frown seemed to cross her face and her emerald eyes narrowed on him.

"Do you think I'm a lady who meets your qualifications?"

"I don't know," he said honestly. "You appear to be a lady."

She bit her lip and he could see her contemplating her thoughts.

"What do you want in a husband?"

Her eyes rose to meet his. "I want a man who accepts me for who I am. Yes, I'm a lady, but there's a wildness inside me that I don't feel has been explored. A part of me that wants to live life to the fullest and not let anything hold me back. I'm not certain that you would consider me a wild woman or a lady."

Stunned, he stared at her. She just admitted she was not a lady. But a wild woman. Jakob didn't know what to think. Was she the woman he wanted to marry?

Martin leaned over and took her hand. "I love that you have a wild side, and I can't wait to explore it."

"Truth or Dare?" Jakob said, knowing how he wanted her to answer.

"Dare," she said with a gasp, her emerald eyes almost taunting him.

"I dare you to let me kiss you," he said.

"All right," she said.

Standing, he walked over to her and lifted her. Without asking, he pulled her into his arms and his lips covered hers.

She tasted of sunshine and clover and everything sweet and innocent. He could tell just from kissing her that she had never been thoroughly kissed before. His tongue swept over her lips and he pushed into her mouth, his tongue dancing with hers and he felt her tremble in his arms.

Taking command of the kiss, he held her tightly and refused to let her escape.

His hand reached for her breast and he felt the swell beneath his hand.

Her lips left his and she opened her eyes and stared at him as she removed his hand. "Mr. Moore, we are not yet man and wife. There are some privileges only available to my husbands."

A grin spread across his face. The woman was definitely an innocent. But a lady would do exactly as she'd done. Still, he felt concerned when she spoke about the wild woman inside her.

What did she mean? And did he want a wild woman for a bride?

CHAPTER 12

"Are you certain you're ready to propose?" Jakob asked.

Martin was driving the wagon into town to pick up Blanche. Today after they showed her the ranch, he wanted to propose to her. The ranch was where they would be living and he thought it would be proper to be able to show their children exactly where he had proposed to their mother.

"I've been ready since day one, but you're the one who has been holding back."

Jakob seemed to have suddenly had second thoughts about whether or not he wanted to marry. It was the first time in years they had not agreed on something.

"You heard her call herself a wild woman. You know I want a lady, not someone who is more of a saloon girl."

"Why? Tell me why you want a proper lady?" Martin asked. "Seems to me you'd like the fact that she's a little on the wild side. Just think what she's going to be like in the bedroom."

Jakob frowned and Martin could see that he liked the idea of her being wild in the bedroom.

"My mother was a perfect lady and that's what I want in a wife."

"Oh, dear God, so you want to marry your mother? That's disgusting."

"No, someone like my mother."

"No one is going to be as perfect as your saintly mother."

"Hey," Jakob said, his face turning red "Watch what you say about my mother."

"I'm not saying anything bad about her. I'm just saying what you expect is not possible. No one is going to meet your expectations. Blanche doesn't have a chance."

The man was impossible if he thought Blanche could be anything like his mother. And Martin had seen that spark in her eye that looked like she was dying to get into trouble. Do something besides act the way a woman should. It was one of the things he liked about her.

He couldn't wait to see her reaction today to their ranch.

"I've said all along that I want a woman who is a lady."

"So you think Blanche is not a lady?"

There was silence for a moment. "Sometimes she seems too perfect. Like she's been taught how to act, but yet she's just dying to break free."

Martin sighed. That was exactly what he saw and yet it didn't bother him. In fact, he wanted to help set her free.

"Then let's not marry her," Martin said, knowing he would be standing in front of the doctor with her in a few days regardless of what Jakob wanted.

Jakob turned and glanced at him, but Martin pretended not to notice.

"If she's not going to make you happy, then we shouldn't marry her."

Martin guided the wagon down the road for the next mile. Jakob said nothing the entire way and Martin was growing fearful that his taunt hadn't worked. He'd said the words just to make Jakob think of what they were letting pass by.

"When we get to the doctor's house, instead of taking her to the ranch, we'll tell her that we've changed our minds. We don't want a wild woman in our bed or being free with us. We want a stuffy lady who will bore us. Who holds tea parties and is dull."

Jakob shook his head at him. "You son of a bitch. You're doing this to me deliberately."

They had reached town. "I'm trying to help you decide. You have about two blocks before we reach the house. If you haven't made your mind up by then, it's over."

A heavy sigh came from Jakob. "All right, let's marry her. But I'm telling you, she's not a lady."

Martin grinned. "She's all I need."

He pulled the wagon to a halt in front of the Sanders's home.

"Let's go get her. I thought the perfect spot to propose would be somewhere near the pond, right before our property goes up into the forest."

"How are we going to get her there?"

"Horseback riding," he said. "And no, don't ask. We don't have a sidesaddle."

Just then the door opened and Blanche lifted her skirts, showing her ankles as she all but skipped down the stairs.

"Hello," she called, her straw hat in her hand.

Jakob glared at Martin and then climbed out of the wagon. He took Blanche in his arms and gave her a brief kiss.

"Jakob," she said, her voice whispery soft. She gave a little giggle. "I'm expecting another kiss from you like that last one."

A grin spread across his face.

"With no touching private areas," she said.

"That's no fun," he said.

"No, but a lady does not allow that kind of fun. And you want a lady," she said, smiling at him.

Oh, the woman had him figured out.

Martin wanted to laugh at the expression on Jakob's face. The man looked stunned and he was glad. Every day, Martin liked Blanche more, and today he couldn't wait to take her out to their ranch and show her their home.

"Martin," she said and threw her arms around him. "I know not how a lady acts, but I am so happy to see you."

"Darling, I'm happy to see you too. And it doesn't matter to me. As long as you're not getting into trouble, I'm happy."

She stepped back and smiled at him. "Let's go. I can't wait to see your ranch."

Martin lifted her and set her in the wagon and then she tilted her head at Jakob.

"Are you coming?"

"Of course," he said, climbing up beside her.

Martin picked up the reins, released the brake and he clicked to the horses. "Giddyup."

The wagon rolled through the streets and then turned and headed toward their ranch. The horses seemed to know instinctively which direction to go and they picked up speed.

"Tell me what kinds of animals you have on your ranch," she said, her emerald eyes sparkling.

Martin had to remind himself to keep his eyes on the horses and the road when all he wanted to do was gaze at Blanche.

Jakob turned and raised his brows at her. "We have cattle, sheep, chickens, and horses. In the summer, Martin raises vegetables in the garden."

"We can a lot of okra, beans, squash, and make pickles. Have you ever done much canning?"

"Oh yes," she said. "Papa and I used to can the veggies from the garden every summer. Do you grow herbs as well?"

Martin turned and gazed at her. "No. But I'm willing to learn."

"Good, they are good for seasoning and also for healing. I make a salve to use on a cow's foot rot. The spring rains seemed to always cause that."

Jakob had been watching the road and he suddenly turned his attention on her, frowning.

"You'll have to show me," Martin said. "I'd like to try some of your salve and see if it works here."

This was not the kind of conversation that a lady would have, but Martin didn't care. He liked that she had asked and even seemed knowledgeable about the subject.

"There are several herbs I grew remedies for. We didn't have the money to go to the doctor and they seemed to help heal us and the animals."

The wagon hit a pothole in the road and the wagon bounced. Blanche slammed into Jakob and he stopped her from moving.

"I'm so sorry, Jakob," she said.

"Darling, I enjoyed the feel of your body slamming into mine."

A blush spread across her face and she glanced away.

Just then Martin turned the horses through the gate and they rolled toward the house down the driveway.

"Wow, look at that home," she said. "In Charleston, we had a big plantation-style home, but nothing like this. This looks more like a real ranch house. I can't wait to see the inside. Did you both build this home?"

"Yes," Martin said. "We built it in mind for a big family. That's why we're ready to marry and settle down. That big house needs little babes running up and down the stairs."

A grin spread across her face.

As soon as the words were out of his mouth Martin thought about the mine disaster. Before he met Blanche, he didn't want to consider marriage and children. What made him think he deserved a wife and children?

Maybe he was wrong to pressure Jakob. Maybe today

was a huge mistake and they shouldn't ask Blanche to marry them.

He turned away, the dark cloud seeming to overcome him, and he felt like he was drowning as the dust cloud, the screams, the sounds of men racing to get out before the walls and roof came crashing down played in his head.

"Martin," Jakob yelled. "Martin. Stop the horses."

Shaking his head, he came back to the present and realized that they were in front of the house.

He pulled the reins and the wagon came to a halt.

"Are you all right?" Blanche asked, laying her hand on his arm.

"I'm fine," he said curtly. What was he thinking? He didn't deserve a happy life.

Turning away from Blanche, he jumped out of the wagon and Jakob helped her alight. How could he tell them he'd changed his mind?

With a sigh, he came around her side of the wagon and she gazed at him. Suddenly she took his arm and gave him the most beautiful smile.

"Show me the house. I can't wait to see what it looks like on the inside," she said. "Jakob can show me the ranch portion. But I want you to show me the house."

No, he didn't deserve Blanche, but he wanted her. God, how he wanted her.

Placing his hand on hers, he led her to the door. "It really needs a woman's touch. We're just a couple of bachelors living here."

He opened the door and together they walked inside. Gazing at her, he watched as her eyes grew large.

"Look at that fireplace. It's huge. I bet it will heat the entire house. And I love the bookshelves on either side. That's great."

The horsehair couch and chair were in a semicircle around the fireplace. They had specifically designed it so that on winter evenings, they could sit in front of the fire and stay warm.

"Behind the living area, we have the dining room. The kitchen is through those doors there."

They had built the house with fire safety in mind. So many homes burned to the ground by fires started in the fireplace or the kitchen. By having a door separating the rooms, they hoped they could put any fire out before it had a chance to burn the entire house.

Jakob opened the door to the kitchen. "Do you know how to cook?"

"Of course," she said. "Who do you think fed my papa and me."

"Good," Jakob said. "Our cooking is not the best."

She smiled. "This is a big kitchen and yet it doesn't feel too big. Do you have a root cellar?"

"Yes," Martin said. "It's behind that door over there."

"Good. We stored our canned goods and root vegetables there."

"Where are the bedrooms?"

"Upstairs," Martin said.

She looked between the two men. "May I see them please?"

"Of course," Jakob said. "We can even try out the bed."

Shaking her head, she shook her finger at him. "Jakob, I think you like to test me."

"Of course," he said, taking her hand and leading her up the stairs. "I'm a man and, honey, I can't wait to strip you naked and hear you moan with pleasure."

Martin watched Blanche and she blushed.

"Not without a ring on my finger," she said.

They walked down the hall.

"This is my bedroom and over here is Martin's," he said and then he led her down to the last door at the end of the hallway. He threw open the door and she gasped.

Martin smiled.

"This will be the bedroom we share with our wife. The other two bedrooms will be for our children. There is a nursery over to the side of the big room where the baby can sleep."

Like she was in a dream, she stepped through the door and gazed around the room. They had designed the room to fit their needs and the needs of their wife. The house had been built just before the mine collapse. At the time, Martin was so ready to marry and have a family, but now suddenly, he was getting cold feet.

Jakob walked in behind her and came up and pulled her up against him.

She gasped.

"Think of what will go on in this room. The times we'll take our bride here. The children we'll create. The love and the births that will occur in this room." His hands came around her and he pulled her arms up overhead as his lips came down on hers.

He kissed her, and Martin, not wanting to be left out, moved in behind her and pulled her against his hard cock straining in his pants with the need to plunge deep inside her.

A moan escaped from her throat as they held her between them, Jakob taking command of her lips, expressing his need as Martin held her in place.

Suddenly he broke the kiss. "This is what we will expect from our wife. Her total surrender as we share her between us."

Blanche's emerald eyes were glazed as she stared at Jakob.

"What's in it for me? You have total control over my body and expect me to surrender. What will I get out of it?"

Speechless, Martin stood there and watched as Jakob didn't really know how to handle this question. The woman was an innocent. She knew nothing about how a man and woman copulated.

"You get two wonderful husbands. Two men who will protect you and our children with their life. Nothing will harm you and one of us all always be by your side."

She licked her lips and he could see she was having trouble breathing. Jakob's kiss had affected her.

"I'll agree to that trade. Show me the ranch," she said in a breathy gasp.

A frown appeared on Jakob's face, but he took her by the hand and the two of them hurried down the stairs.

Martin took one last look at the room they'd prepared before he closed the door and rushed after them.

When he caught up, they were in the barn. The ranch

hands had three horses saddled and ready to go. On the way out the door, he'd grabbed the picnic basket.

"The barn holds all the animals, but we'd like to take you out to the pasture and let you see the mares and have lunch down by the creek."

"We're riding?" Her emerald eyes grew large and a big smile crossed her face.

"Yes," Jakob said, surprised by her eagerness.

"Which horse am I riding?" she asked.

"The sorrel," Martin said.

She walked up to the horse and ran her hand over its nose and slid her hands down its neck. "I used to own a horse that looked a lot like this one. She was my favorite and we use to ride the land together. Oh, how I miss her."

The wistfulness in her voice was urgent and he understood her missing the animal.

Martin smiled. If they married, he knew what he was giving her for a wedding gift. A horse of her own.

"I'm sorry we don't have a sidesaddle," Jakob said. "I'll get you one."

"Don't bother," she said stepping up into the stirrups, she threw her leg over the horse, her dress riding up, showing her ankles.

"If my ankles bother you, don't look," she said and gave the horse a little kick. "Sidesaddles are dangerous. The combination of sidesaddle and long skirts means the lady cannot fall clear of the horse and is likely to be trampled. It can also hurt the horse with so much weight being unbalanced. As ranchers, I'm surprised you men don't know that. Isn't safety your top concern for me and your animals?"

In astonishment, Jakob and Martin watched her ride out of the barn. The woman knew how to ride a horse, and how to make them feel uneducated.

"We better go," Jakob said. "Our bride is showing me she's not always a lady."

"Thank God," Martin said.

They each climbed onto their horse and rode out of the barn. She was already flying across the fields.

"Look at her," Jakob said. "That is not how a lady comports herself."

"No, and isn't she beautiful," Martin said watching her. "I had a little spell while we were driving here and I decided I couldn't marry her. But watching her now, I have to have her. Come on, let's catch up. It's time to ask her to marry us."

Martin knew that Jakob would now be questioning everything, but he didn't care. Yes, he was still scared and insecure. If he didn't still have moments of fear exploding inside him, he would have no questions about marrying her. But even now, he dreaded the next time he would go back in time and relive the mine explosion all over again.

Finally, she began to slow the horse, walking her and petting her, and Martin would guess, talking to the animal. The horse shook its head as if it were agreeing with her.

They galloped up alongside her.

"Good day, gentlemen," she said. "You have no idea how much I've missed this. Thank you for letting me ride this wonderful animal."

Jakob shook his head and Martin hoped he wasn't about to lecture her on conduct for a woman.

"See that creek over there?" Martin asked. "Let's ride over there and we can have our lunch."

She pressed the sides of the horse and once again they were off and running. Her glorious auburn hair was flying out in the wind, her trim ankles were out and her dress billowed on the back of the horse.

All he knew was that he'd never seen such a carefree rider who knew how to handle the animal. It was like she and the horse were one. It was like an auburn angel riding the wind.

She reached the pond and let the horse have rein in order to have a drink. When they caught up to her, she grinned

"What a wonderful day," she said, as her feet dropped to the ground.

"Where should we have our picnic?" Martin asked.

Frowning, Jakob sat in his saddle staring at her. "Where did you learn to ride like that?"

"My papa," she said. "No saddle, no dress, just me in a pair of pants riding every day until he felt like he could let me ride alone. He started me when I was just four."

Martin slid off his horse and pulled off the picnic basket from his horse. He spread a blanket and then set out the food.

Jakob swung his leg over the saddle and slid down.

After they ate, they planned to talk to her about their expectations and then they would offer to marry her.

After everything was ready, Blanche sank to the ground

beside him. Jakob took the other side of her.

While it was a wonderful idea to wait until after they ate, right now Martin felt like his stomach was up in his throat and he couldn't swallow. Yes, he had his doubts, but after seeing her ride the range today, all he could think about was ripping that dress off her and taking her right here on the blanket.

If she accepted their offer, after they were married, he would take her right here in the open.

"Blanche, we've talked about what we want in a woman. Tell us what you want in a husband."

"Everything," she said. "Everything you've spoken about is what I want. This place, this land, this just all seems so perfect."

Jakob frowned. "Do you realize that if you disobey us, we're going to paddle that pert little behind of yours? That we will spank you for pleasure and for punishment."

A frown appeared and then she smiled. "I've never been spanked. My papa didn't believe in it. While I don't understand why you would want to spank me, I'm not unwilling to try it. But if you spank me for punishment, it had better be something that is really, really bad. I'm not going to accept you beating me."

Martin felt tense. He really didn't like to spank his woman for anything other than pleasure. "Darling, when my hand hits your back end, it's going to make you feel so good. If we had neighbors, they would hear your moans."

Stunned, she glanced at Martin and smiled. "You'll have to show me because I've never been spanked by anyone. I didn't know you could get pleasure from punishment."

Jakob moved in closer to her. "I'm going to enjoy punishing you. It gives me such joy when you disobey and I get to paddle you. I promise never to hurt you, but you will remember what you did wrong."

Martin could tell she was confused and he didn't want her to focus on the punishment side of things. He wanted her to think about the pleasure they would give her.

"Darling, we promise as your husbands that we will make you enjoy sex so much, you're going to be asking us to take you."

A smile spread across her face. "I have no clue as to what you're talking about. I know so little about the sex act."

"We can't wait to teach you, but before we begin…"

Martin rose from the blanket and was down on one knee. "Blanche, will you marry me and Jakob and let us spend our days making you happy. Will you love and cherish us until death do we part?"

Her mouth fell open and she grinned. "Yes. Oh, yes. I was beginning to think you would never ask."

She threw her arms around Martin and the doubts began to immediately plague him. He didn't deserve her. He didn't deserve to have children. He was a monster, and yet all he could think about was Blanche.

Jakob came over and she pulled him into her arms. "My men. My husbands. I will do my best to be the best wife possible for both of you. A lady in the day to make Jakob happy and my usual wild self at night in our bed."

Martin groaned. If she could do that, they would indeed be very happily married.

CHAPTER 13

*T*oday she was marrying the best-looking men in town. And they owned a ranch. Everything she dreamed of was beginning to come true. Everything.

And it was hard to believe that traveling from Charleston to Treasure Falls had been the best thing she'd ever done.

No, she didn't love her husbands, but then she didn't believe they loved her yet either. Hopefully, they would all come around. Jakob was a strong man with a domineering personality. There was something about him she couldn't quite figure out yet. Why was he obsessed with marrying a lady?

Could she be the woman he desired?

Martin was a gentle, kind soul who reminded her of a big teddy bear. Though something bothered him. Hopefully, once they were married, she would learn why he often looked sad. The other day, he seemed to just disappear inside himself.

Today, six couples with an extra bridegroom would all say "I do" in front of each other. It would be one big ceremony. One big party. Something she'd never attended. This wedding would be her first. And she couldn't help but wonder what she would learn today.

This morning, Mary and Daisy and she had sat on the bed and asked each other if they were making the right decision and each woman agreed this was right for them. Each woman was happy with the two men who had chosen her and each woman knew that after today, they would only see each other when they could. The months of living together were over and they were each beginning a new chapter of her life.

A chapter she hoped would bring her happiness. If only she could continue to be the prim-and-proper woman Jakob wanted. And Martin, she just wanted to hold him, assure him, and make him realize that everything would be all right.

She would protect him like he promised to protect her and their children.

After she announced her engagement, Aunt Grace had spoken to her about how marriage was with two men. She had no idea how marriage to one man would be, so this was not shocking to her.

And learning how sex happened with two men, she was a little nervous today.

All she wanted to do was be the best wife possible for both of her men. To make them happy. To please them.

Blanche stood in her new purple dress waiting for her turn to walk down the stairs and her two men would meet her there, and once all the women were downstairs, the ceremony would begin.

Aunt Grace stood by the stairs. She hugged Blanche. "Good luck, Blanche."

"Thank you," Blanche said, feeling the tears well in her eyes. Aunt Grace was the closest figure she had to a mother.

Blanche began the descent and saw her two men waiting for her at the bottom. They grinned at her and when she reached them, they hugged her.

"Happy wedding day," Martin said.

"Happy wedding day," Jakob replied. "I can't wait to get you home tonight."

She smiled at them and her nerves kicked in. Tonight, she would learn what they expected from her. Tonight was their wedding night.

Each man took one of her arms and placed it on his and they walked over to stand in front of Dr. Sanders, who would be saying the vows once all the couples were gathered.

The memory of standing on the porch of her home with a gun pointed at the new owner and the sheriff came to mind, and she almost giggled. As much as she missed her old home, her animals, and living there, she had so much hope that after today, she would once again have a good place to live. A ranch with farm animals and maybe she could get another dog.

She loved the feel of a dog, and how when the world seemed ready to implode, they were there by her side, licking her hand and gazing at her with those big soft brown eyes.

The doctor stood before them and began the words that would join them together as man and wife. Staring at her husbands, she repeated her vows.

The doctor grinned at them. "Gentlemen, you may kiss your bride."

First Martin leaned in and kissed her, making her knees weak. Then Jakob pulled her into his arms and covered her lips molding her body against his. When he finally released her, she felt almost faint.

The man knew how to kiss. And one thing she already knew about him was that he needed to be in control. How long could she let him control her?

"Be a good lady and we'll be happy," he whispered as he leaned his head against her forehead.

Oh, that was like a taunt. Did he not realize that now she wanted to show him she could be anyone she wanted to be? But it was their wedding day.

"Always," she said, knowing that wasn't possible.

The doctor glanced at the group of them. "How wonderful. Now we know the town of Treasure Falls will continue. May you be blessed with many children and long lives together."

The dinner seemed to last forever with many toasts to happiness and children. Finally, her men took her by the arm.

"We need to get home," Martin said.

"Are you all packed?" Jakob asked

"Yes," she said, suddenly feeling very nervous. "I must

tell the girls good-bye."

She walked over to Mary and hugged her. "I'm going to miss you."

"We'll see each other in town," Mary said.

Daisy walked up.

"Daisy, I'm getting my dream. Another ranch. Promise me you'll come see me," she said.

"You know I will. Soon," Daisy told her. "Be happy."

"You too," she said, hugging Daisy.

"I hope so," she said. "Come see me."

Out of the corner of her eye, she saw Alice. The woman hated her and yet Blanche tried her best to be friendly with her. "Good-bye, Alice."

"I hope your men realize what a tramp they're getting. Did you tell them, you were pregnant?"

Chills went through Blanche. Why did the woman think she was pregnant? She'd been sick and even thought that Alice poisoned her.

"Alice, I'm not a tramp. I'm not pregnant. Honestly, I thought you poisoned me," she said calmly, trying her best to act like the lady her husbands expected.

"They'll soon learn the truth about you," Alice said with a sneer as she turned and walked away.

It was all Blanche could do not to go after the woman and punch her. But she didn't want to ruin her wedding and everyone else's. Alice had chosen to return to Charleston. Hopefully, she would never see her again.

The woman walked away and Blanche's men came up to her.

"Let's go," Jakob said grinning.

The man was so eager to take her virginity. They could hardly wait to get her into bed and she was still a little nervous about being taken by two men.

"My carpetbag is right there," she said, pointing to the small carrier Mrs. Newton had given her before she left Charleston.

She hugged Aunt Grace and the woman smiled at her. "Have a great night."

Blanche blushed clear to her toes. She couldn't believe the woman was openly talking about their wedding night.

"Thanks for everything," she told the woman and then took Martin's arm as they walked out the door.

When they reached the wagon, Martin once again took the reins. When they were about a block from the house, Jakob reached under her skirts.

Could the man not wait?

"What are you doing?"

"Removing your bloomers. You will no longer need them," he said. "In fact, we want you to remain naked this first week. That way we can take you anytime, anywhere."

"But…what if we have guests?"

"We won't," Martin said.

"This is not how a lady would act," she said, wondering how she could be what Jakob wanted when he was the one who was asking her to do things that were not civil.

He put them to his nose and breathed deeply of her bloomers. She watched with fascination. Men were certainly different from women.

He smiled. "I want a lady in public and a whore in the bedroom. You'll soon learn."

Cool air went up her skirts. She felt almost naked without them. If only he knew that she had not had a nice pair of bloomers until Mrs. Newton purchased them for her.

They were silent on the drive to the house, each of them anticipating the night's activities.

When they pulled up in front of the house, Blanche began to grow more nervous. She had learned about sex by watching the animals on the ranch. Her father had never spoken to her about what happened between a man and a woman.

Martin pulled the wagon to a halt, set the brake, and then turned to help Blanche from the wagon. Only this time, he scooped her up into his arms and didn't set her down.

"I'll be in shortly," Jakob said as he drove the wagon to the back of the house.

"What are we doing?"

"I'm carrying you over the threshold, darling. It's good luck when a groom carries his bride over the threshold."

"Oh," she said swallowing

He opened the door and carried her in. When they were inside, he let her body slide down his and she could feel his very, hard, rigid penis against her womanly parts.

A warmth began to bloom inside her. She licked her lips nervously.

"What now?" she asked.

"Strip," he told. "I want you naked in the next five minutes."

"But what about Jakob?"

Martin smiled. "Oh, he'll be so excited to see you naked when he comes in. Now strip."

Blanche swallowed nervously and began to remove her clothes.

CHAPTER 14

Blanche's hands were shaking as she tried to reach the buttons on the back of her dress.

"I can't reach the buttons," she said, thinking of how Mary and Daisy had helped her dress.

Martin came over and quickly undid the clasps.

Swallowing apprehensively, she watched as he moved in front of her.

"Keep going," he said.

As much as she'd prepared for tonight, you would think she would not have wedding night jitters, but that wasn't true. This was her first time and she wanted to please her husbands.

No matter what, she wanted this marriage to work and that began tonight. She knew Jakob had doubts about her, and to an extent, she wanted to please him, but Martin...he was the one she thought cared the most about her.

Slowly she peeled the dress down her shoulders. No man had ever seen her naked. No one.

She stepped out of the dress and carefully laid it aside.

"The rest," Martin told her.

The door swung open and Jakob strolled in. His eyes widened when he saw her standing there in front of them in her chemise.

"Don't stop," Jakob told her. "We can't wait to fuck you."

The word was harsh and while she knew that's what they were going to do, she still wanted her first time to be a loving experience. She wanted them to want her, but also cherish her.

"This is our wedding night," she said. "I want this to be a perfect evening. I'm going to go upstairs to our room. Give me five minutes and I'll be waiting for you."

She grabbed her dress and marched up the stairs. In the background, she heard Martin scolding Jakob.

"She wants hearts and flowers and was perfectly fine until you came in and said you wanted to fuck her. Girls have dreams about their wedding night. It's the night they give their bodies to their husband."

Jakob knew the moment the words were out of his mouth and her emerald eyes narrowed she was not happy.

"I know," Jakob said. "I got carried away."

"Do better," Martin told him. "If you're so damn determined to have a lady, then you need to be more of a proper gentleman."

Smiling, she slipped into the big bedroom. Quickly she removed the rest of her clothes. She pulled back the quilt and climbed into bed.

Taking a deep breath, she tried to relax. She was a

married woman, and tonight she would give herself to her husbands. Only she had no idea what that meant.

Martin and Jakob walked through the door. They begin to remove their clothes. First, their shirts and Blanche stared, mesmerized. Martin's chest was rippled with muscles and his biceps were large and strong and she knew that he could protect her.

Jakob was tall, and though his chest was not as muscled as Martin's, he looked like he could fight an entire army. His fists were large, his arms were large and the way he carried himself was like a tough fighter ready for battle.

Sitting in a chair across the room, Martin pulled his boots off and his socks. Standing, he unbuttoned his pants and let them slide to the floor. He wore nothing underneath. Standing before her, he was naked, his cock hard and long and she felt a moment of panic.

How in the hell could she take him into her body?

Jakob removed his boots and unbuttoned his pants. His flesh was not the darker color like Martin's, but rather white. And his cock was long and hard like a spear.

They moved toward the bed and she felt a brief panic, but quickly controlled it.

"You are our wife. Tomorrow when I tell you to do something, I expect you to obey," Martin said to her.

"I forget that you're a lady and not used to rough talk. I'll do better," Jakob said and she felt amazed. It was a roundabout apology and yet she felt like it was sincere.

Maybe they were making progress.

Suddenly Jakob pulled the quilt back and she lay there

naked before them. She tried to cover her breasts and womanly parts, but Martin pulled her hands away.

"You're our wife. We want to see your beauty. We know you're nervous. This is your first time, but it's our duty as your husbands to make certain that you enjoy the pleasure we're going to give you."

Heat spread through her at the thought of them giving her pleasure.

The sun had sunk below the horizon, and in the light of the oil lanterns, she gazed at her men.

Staring up at them, she frowned. "Is this going to hurt?"

"If you're a virgin, maybe a little," Jakob said.

"No doubt, I can tell you're an innocent who does not know the ways of men. But you'll soon learn."

The thought of them putting their cocks inside her frightened her. But she was strong and she could do this.

"Tonight is only the beginning. We'll train you exactly how we like sex. Soon, you'll know our commands and what we want."

Jakob crawled up beside her. "Darling, I can't wait until we both take you. But that's going to have to wait. Tonight, we're going to give you pleasure. And if you're not crying out our names, then we haven't done our job."

It seemed odd that he expected her to cry out his name. It seemed odd that he wasn't certain she was a virgin. Well, he would soon learn the truth.

Jakob's mouth came down over hers. She liked his kisses. They were strong and demanding and his lips took control only requiring her surrender. As his lips moved over her mouth, she felt Martin's hands moving over her breasts, trailing down her stomach to her womanly area. His fingers touched her intimately and she felt a rush of heat spiral through her.

A moan escaped from her as he tweaked the button between her legs and she tried to raise her hips seeking his hand for even more. The feelings she was experiencing were something she'd never felt. It was an intense pleasure that had her craving more of something she didn't even understand.

Jakob broke the kiss and gazed down at her. "What are you feeling?"

Gasping, she clenched the quilt in her hands. "Martin is doing something to me that is arousing something and yet I really like it."

"Good," Jakob said as he leaned down and took her nipple in his mouth. He pulled the end, sending heat simmering from her breasts all the way to her center. Oh God, this was so much more than she expected.

His teeth nipped her nipple and she cried out, not from pain, but from the fire that shot through her.

"Jakob," she cried.

"Yes, darling," he said. "We've only just started and already you're crying out my name."

Martin moved down by her feet and she couldn't help but wonder what he was doing.

Then he spread her legs and gazed at her in the most intimate of places.

"Martin," she cried. "What are you doing?"

"Oh, Jakob, she's got the sweetest little pussy. And I'm going to taste it."

Shock rumbled through her as he spread her innermost lips and he placed his mouth on her center and kissed her. Shockwaves of pleasure pulsed through her as she gripped the bed sheets.

"Blanche, we're going to taste you in every way. And if we do it right, you're going to enjoy every second of Martin's mouth on your sweet cunny."

She didn't understand what they were doing or sometimes even what they were saying to her, but she was loving the feelings Martin was creating and even Jakob as his mouth returned to her nipples. Dear God, pressure was building inside her that had her lifting her hips, needing more, wanting more.

As Martin's tongue lapped at her inner lips, she gripped the quilt, needing something she didn't understand. And yet, she felt decadent with her legs spread, giving Martin even more access.

This was not how she thought of a wedding night. This was not what she expected. It was better. Desire as hot as melted butter filled her and she moaned.

As Martin's tongue continued to lick her, she felt his finger probe her back entrance.

"Martin," she cried. "No."

Slap! His hand found her pussy and he slapped it hard enough to send a rush of heat through her. Stunned at the feelings, she gasped and tried to roll away.

Slap!

"We are your husbands. Your body is ours. You don't tell us what to do. Soon, not tonight, you will experience more than my finger in your ass."

His fingers were toying with her privates and a hot slick sheen of her essence coated his digits.

"Do it again," Jakob said, raising from her breasts. "Slap that pussy. I can feel she's getting ready to come."

Slap!

The world exploded around her and she clinched Martin's fingers as he slid inside her pussy and one in her ass as she screamed her pleasure.

"Oh," she cried, the sound resounding in the room.

"That's it, darling," Jakob said. "Your first orgasm."

As she lay there, her breathing quick and shallow, the world seemed to right itself and she gasped as Martin moved up the bed to lie on the other side of her.

They moved her and sandwiched her between them. The feeling of their big hard bodies surrounded her and she loved the feel of their naked skin against her own.

"Did you like it when I spanked your pussy?" Martin asked.

The pleasure had been so intense, and yet it seemed so unnatural when his finger rubbed her ass. But when he spanked her pussy, a rush of heat consumed her unlike anything she'd ever felt.

"We're learning what excites you. Nothing is wrong here in the bedroom. Nothing that gives the three of us pleasure. So be honest with us."

"It's all so new. Yes, I enjoyed it very much. It was a shock and then the heat would overcome me."

They pulled her into an embrace between them.

"Whatever we enjoy is not wrong," Martin said, gazing into her eyes as he kissed her softly on the lips. "We're your men, your husbands, and we want to make certain you enjoy sex with us."

Moving over the top of her, Jakob knelt between her legs.

"I'm going to take your maidenhead," Jakob said. "If you have one."

Sure, she could argue with him and tell him she didn't like his tone, but then that would ruin everything. She'd wait. She'd get her chance.

And he would know she did not appreciate his doubts.

Jakob rolled onto his back and then Martin lifted her and placed the entrance to her cunny right on top of Jakob's cock. The size of his cock was large, much bigger than Martin's, sending fear spiraling through her, and yet, she knew her body would adjust to his size.

"Jakob," she said, as he began to fiddle with her clit, teasing her, making her want him even more than she did, "when you take my maidenhood, you're going to apologize to me."

A grin spread across his face as he realized she was calling him out on his maddening taunt.

"If you're a virgin, I will," he said. "I'll even make certain you have another orgasm."

"That I'm getting, regardless," she said, feeling certain that Martin would not leave her feeling frustrated.

Jakob lifted her hips and slapped her on the ass.

"You're getting a little brazen, bride. Don't make me spank you again," he warned her.

"Darling, I'll always be forthright with you. Even if you do spank me," she told him. "If I want to say something, I will. If I disagree with you, I will. Even if you decide to spank me."

He raised her hips and slapped her ass again. "I'm going to love giving you spankings."

Her hips were burning, but it wasn't a painful burn, but more of a sensuous heat. A heat she quickly learned she enjoyed.

Martin was behind her and she felt his hands come around and squeeze her nipples. "Blanche, it's time. Time for us to make you ours."

Jakob placed his cock at her entrance. "The moment of truth."

"I'll expect that apology," she said.

With a shove, he plunged into her and she felt him hit the wall of resistance.

"Damn," he said. "She's a virgin."

"I could have told you that," Martin said.

Blanche knew the pain was coming and tried to relax. With a quick shove, he broke the wall of her virginity.

For a moment, she felt a stinging sensation. Jakob waited, giving her a few seconds to adjust.

"Well, darling, I owe you an apology. You're more of a lady than I thought. But now, I'm going to make you into a whore. My whore. Martin's whore. We're going to train you, but we'll never share you with another man. You're ours. Repeat it back to me."

"I'm yours," she said with a gasp as he began to move again. "Jakob."

"Soon you're going to be screaming my name," he said, grasping her hips and bringing her pussy to meet his cock.

Martin's hands were on her breasts as he tugged and pinched her nipples, spreading passion through her body. With a moan, she closed her eyes and let her head roll back.

"Open your eyes, Blanche. I want to see the desire in your gaze. I want to stare at you when you come. I want to know we made you feel this way. Nothing else."

As she opened her eyes, her breathing was harsh as she felt Jakob rubbing his finger at her back entrance. She tried not to panic as he slid his finger into her ass, swirling it around. A burst of need went off inside her like a bomb and she leaned back on Martin.

Never had she imagined a man's finger bringing her so much pleasure there. All she knew was that it made him feel incredibly tight in her pussy. Again, the pressure grew and expanded, and while part of her wanted to escape, part of her was eager and needed more.

"Don't come," Jakob said.

"Why not?" she asked, knowing she taunted him. Knowing he wanted an obedient wife, but she wasn't that kind of girl. Oh no, she was going to defy him often.

"Because I said not to," Jakob said and smacked her on the ass, which only made it more difficult not to come.

"Do I have to wait for you?"

"Yes," he groaned.

"My hot virgin, pussy wasn't enough to make you come?"

He stared down at her and she could see that her words were making him push faster.

"Your cock is so hard. Let me come," she cried. "Come for me, Jakob."

"Damn, woman," he said with a groan. "Come now."

It was then that Jakob's hand landed on her ass, his finger buried deep inside her and she screamed as her body convulsed. Panting, she never imagined what Jakob said would be true. That she would loudly proclaim her pleasure.

Leaning back against Martin, he let her rest until her breathing began to slow. All she wanted to do was roll over and take a nap.

"Blanche, now it's my turn. I can't wait to bury my cock so far in your cunny that you're screaming for relief."

Already her body was beginning to stir. Was he mad? How could she want it again?

"Watching you fuck Jakob, I'm rock hard and ready to explode. This is going to be hard and fast."

What did he mean by hard and fast? He pulled her to the edge of the bed. Suddenly he grabbed her legs and spread her wide, opening her to his cock. In amazement, she watched as his cock slid in and out of her pussy. Once again, the pressure was mounting inside her and she clenched his cock.

In that moment, she knew what he meant by hard and fast. After having come twice, she was shocked at how, once again, her body responded, her muscles constricting around and gripping him.

"Oh my, she's tight and I can feel my seed racing to explode."

Jakob chuckled and leaned down and kissed her on the

lips. The feel of his mouth on hers, the way his tongue glided over her lips and slipped between them, sent fire racing through her body.

Reaching up, she put her arms around his shoulders and held him to her. Her tongue danced with his, refusing to concede. Refusing to let him take full control. Oh no, she wanted more.

Another orgasm began to build within her. She lifted her hips to meet his thrusts, wanting as much of him as she could take. Tonight was her wedding night, and so far, it had been better than she'd ever expected. Better than she thought possible, and she wasn't ready for it to end. Even after both men took her, she wanted more.

Each man felt different. Each man's cock gave her pleasure, and she knew she was about to come. Releasing Jakob's lips, her breathing was hard.

"Can I please come?" she gasped between breaths, knowing she couldn't hold back much longer.

"Yes," Martin said. "Come now."

This time, the explosion raced through her, sending her spiraling out of control. Screaming, she grabbed the sheets to hold onto while Jakob held her in his arms, rocking her. Martin stared into her eyes and she felt like they were connected as one.

Suddenly his seed exploded inside her and flooded the walls of her pussy. He continued to hold her legs up as they both tried to regain their breath.

"Don't let my seed run out. Tonight maybe we've created a baby. A girl with your looks or a boy to name after Jakob and me."

Amazed, she lay there for a moment. A child. Oh, yes, she would love it if she became pregnant tonight. A family of their own.

A child she would never leave or give up for any reason. Nothing could drag her away from a child of her own.

If this was married life, then she couldn't be happier.

CHAPTER 15

*T*his morning as the sun peeked into the room, Jakob slowly awoke. The feel of Blanche draped across his body, a welcome respite. The woman liked to taunt him, tease him, and he realized she would never back down.

And sometimes, he wondered if he really wanted her to. But he did want a lady. And Blanche was a lady, he hoped. Though he only had a few hours of sleep last night, he felt rested enough to want his new wife again.

This time without her sass.

It wasn't until he met Martin and they shared a prostitute that he considered the idea of sharing a woman. Though they were not blood brothers, Jakob considered Martin the brother he never had.

And he understood Martin's anguish unlike anyone else. The man lived in fear of reliving the mine collapse.

Martin couldn't wait to get Blanche pregnant, but Jakob

would like some time alone with her and Martin. Enough time for him to decide on whether to stay or go.

Yes, he wanted children. A baby suckling at her breast. A toddler running through the house. Children playing outside.

But not yet. Not until after he'd trained her to do as they commanded for her own safety. Not until he was certain he was staying here in Treasure Falls.

Martin stirred and rolled toward their woman.

"What a night," he said softly. "That was the best night of my life."

Jakob laughed. "It's time to wake her and begin her training."

Even the thought of them taking her together was enough to make him hard as a rock. It would be a slow process, but as soon as she was ready, they would shove their cocks up both her holes.

"Wake her up," Martin said as he laid his mouth over hers, consuming her lips as Jakob watched.

His hand went between her legs and he stroked her clit. Her eyes flew open and she moaned, wrapping her hands around Martin's head, holding his mouth to hers.

Slowly he broke the kiss.

Jakob was so glad she seemed to enjoy sex. At the beginning, he'd been afraid, but then she slowly relaxed.

"My husband," she said softly. "I love waking up in your arms."

Martin grinned.

"Good morning, Jakob," she said softly, arching her back. "How are you this morning?"

"Ready to fuck you," he said.

A laugh came from between her lips. "Did you not get enough last night?"

"Not possible," Martin said. "Roll over. On your elbows with your ass sticking up in the air."

Jakob knew Martin was about to prepare her to receive the first butt plug and they wanted to shave her. See that sweet pussy between her legs.

"Agreed. Not possible," Jakob told her as he watched Martin maneuver her into place. Today they would begin her training.

Slowly she moved, her emerald eyes glazed with passion.

He reached out and twisted her clit. "Oh, darling, you're going to enjoy this morning."

"What are we going to do?" she asked.

"We're going to show you some new things. Some things that we hope you will enjoy as much as we do."

"And what is that?" she asked.

"Wait and see. It's a surprise."

Martin crawled out of the bed and a frown crossed her face. "Where are you going? I want you here with me."

A chuckle came from Martin.

"He'll be back," Jakob reeled as he continued to stroke her clit, causing her to moan, wanting to shove his hard cock in her sweet pussy.

Martin returned with a jar of ointment and the first of the plugs they were going to use on her ass.

Opening the jar, he spread the goo on the plug and then he turned to Blanche. "In order to prepare you to take the both of us, we're going to have you wear a butt plug for several days."

"A what?"

"It's called a butt plug and it stretches you so that you can accept our cocks easily in your ass."

"Oh," she said. "Will it hurt?"

"I don't think so."

Martin crawled up on the bed behind her and spread her ass cheeks. Her head whipped around to him. "What are you doing?"

He held up the plug and showed it to her. "This is the smallest one, and when we reach the fourth, one you'll be ready to take both of us at the same time."

Her mouth dropped open. "No, you're not going to shove that in me."

She whirled back around, placing her buttocks on the bed. He had not expected her reaction.

"Turn around, Blanche, or I'll take you over my knee and spank you," Jakob promised.

She glared at him. "You really like to threaten me with a spanking."

Jakob grinned as she went back up on her knees.

"I'll make certain you enjoy it," Martin told her.

Martin rubbed some of the ointment on her puckered hole and then he began to push the pointed plug into her sphincter.

She tensed, and at Martin's nod, Jakob removed his hand from her clit. He reached down and slapped her on her pussy. "Relax, darling, don't make me spank you."

"There you go again," she said.

A moan escaped her and Jakob realized when he popped her pussy, it increased her excitement, and like a flower, she slowly opened for Martin.

"Aargh," she said. "It feels so big."

"Relax," Martin said as he twisted the plug.

"Relax or I'm going to pull you over my knee and paddle that white ass of yours until it's pink," Jakob said, leaning down. With his fingers on her clit, she began to move her hips and when she did, Martin slipped the rest of the plug into her.

"Now, I'm going to fuck you," Martin told her.

Jakob wished he was between Blanche's legs, but Martin had awakened her, so he would go first. But as soon as he was finished, Jakob would take his turn.

But in the meantime...

"Martin," she cried. "I'm so full. Please, make me come."

A moan escaped from her, and she rocked back and forth with Martin pumping into her. Already she gazed at him like a cat in heat. Like she wanted more.

Jakob leaned in again and pinched her nipples. He rose and faced her. "Suck my cock."

Placing his penis on her lips, she opened her mouth and he shoved it in. "Suck on the end. Run your tongue around the head and don't let your teeth touch it."

She gazed up at him, her emerald gaze shining.

Martin began to pummel her pussy, his face tightening as he held onto her hips, slamming into her again and again, bumping against the butt plug.

Jakob couldn't wait until they both took her at the same

time. Soon, very soon, they would claim her together. Twisting her nipples, her moans increased, and he knew she was close.

Martin shoved into her wet pussy and slapped her on the ass. Just the sounds of their fucking turned Jakob on so hard, he feared he would explode before he had the chance to experience her once again.

Slowly and methodically, she stroked his penis with her tongue, running it about the edge. Knowing he couldn't last much longer, he grabbed her face and held her head in place as he plunged into her mouth over and over. Finally, he exploded into her mouth.

Though she was inexperienced, he knew that was some of the best sex he'd ever had.

"Swallow it," he told her as he released her. Her head sank down onto the bed using her hair as a pillow.

Her breathing was erratic and Martin pummeled his cock into her sweet pussy. He gave her another slap on the ass, turning her white cheeks pink.

"Now you can come," Martin groaned as he held her hips tight and plunged into her wet soaking pussy.

A scream tore from her mouth as her body convulsed. "Oh, Martin."

Before she could come down completely from her climax, Jakob took Martin's position. Rising from the bed, he slipped behind her. Once again, he slapped her wet pussy, reigniting the nerves centered there, and then plunged his cock into her.

"Jakob," she screamed.

"Fuck me," he told her and she raised her ass higher allowing him to go deeper.

He thumped the plug in her ass and she moaned as he shoved his cock into her. Rough and not gentle, he gripped her hips, shoving into her cunny as he drove his cock home, pounding into her.

This was exactly what they both needed. She was a tempting morsel and he needed to show her he had all the control.

This was his woman, his wife, and he wanted his scent impaled upon her to drive other men away. Only with Martin would he share her. She was theirs and he felt this urge to mark her with his scent.

Much too soon, he could feel his seed building and knew it wouldn't be long before he came.

"Who do you belong to?" he gasped.

"You and Martin," she moaned.

"Don't you ever forget it," he said as he popped her ass with his hand.

"Jakob," she cried.

"Come for me," he said as he pushed one last time into her cunt. "Come now."

With a scream, her body squeezed his cock, wringing every last drop of his come from him. She convulsed with the passion they created as he collapsed on top of her.

Martin stroked her face as the three of them fell together onto the bed with Blanche lying between them.

She lay spent, unable to move, but Jakob knew they were not finished with her yet.

They all lay there, waiting for their breathing to slow,

their hearts to return to normal, and their bodies to slowly return to earth.

"I didn't know marriage was like this," she said with a gasp. "I think I'm going to like being married."

The men chuckled.

"There is one more thing we need to do," Jakob said.

"Roll over," Martin said as he rose from the bed.

Jakob pulled her up into his arms while Martin prepared everything.

When he returned to the bed, she gazed up at him. "What are you doing?"

"I'm going to shave your pussy. No more hair between your legs."

Suddenly he slapped the shaving cream between her legs.

"Martin," she gasped.

Then he let the brush spread the cream over her lady parts. She lifted her hips trying to escape the feel of the brushes spreading over her.

"Darling, I think you're enjoying what Martin's doing," Jakob whispered in her ear.

"It feels good, but I'm also terrified he's going to cut me."

"Oh no, Martin would never harm you," he told her.

In a couple of swipes, the hair was gone and she was bare.

Sitting up she gazed down. "It's clean."

"Yes, it is," Jakob said. "Now for your reward."

Martin put his lips on her shaven pussy and she tensed and then cried out.

"I'm going to come again," she said.

Jakob chuckled. "Yes, you are."

He held her, while in a matter of moments, Martin's lips had her screaming out his name. Jakob watched as his friend slowly enticed Blanche. And he knew their wife had enjoyed her wedding night.

CHAPTER 16

*L*ater, that morning, Blanche stood naked as the day she was born in the kitchen cooking pancakes. Cooking was something she enjoyed, and now she had a delightful kitchen that was fully stocked.

And two very hungry men.

It seemed their pantry at home was never fully stocked. Quickly she pushed the thoughts of home out of her mind. She would never return. That was in the past. It was best to focus on the here and now, and not what was once her home.

Sliding a pancake onto a plate, she handed it to Jakob. "The butter and syrup are on the table."

"Thank you, wife," he said.

"No more having to eat our own cooking," Martin said.

She handed Martin a plate with a pancake on it. It was almost noon. They had spent the morning in bed with them explaining to her how their life would be. It seemed as long as she obeyed them, they would be happy.

If only she could control this wild streak in her that seemed to like to get into trouble.

Sadly, Blanche was not one for rules unless you wanted them to be broken. It would take time, but they would soon learn that she made her own decisions and rules.

"I'm sure your cooking is very good. And you do realize that there will be times when you have to cook again," she said. "If I'm nine months pregnant or recovering from birth, someone is going to have to cook besides me."

"I can't wait," Martin said. "I'll gladly cook during that time, but don't expect it to be this good."

She smiled and leaned down and kissed the top of his head.

Jakob continued eating, he didn't say a word and she wondered if he wanted children as badly as she did. As badly as Martin seemed to want them. Why hadn't she thought to ask this question before she married him?

The two men gobbled up their pancakes and she smiled. They obviously were enjoying them.

"Luckily, my cooking will only be for a short time," Martin said. "Let's just say that Jakob is not a great cook."

Jakob turned to glance at Martin. "Hey, we had food, didn't we? No one starved."

She giggled.

"After breakfast, we might have to take you right here in the kitchen. Spread you on the table and let you experience another orgasm today."

"Oh, I'm already starting to harden again," Martin said, leaning back after finishing his plate.

She could feel her cheeks brighten. "I was planning on spending the day unpacking."

It felt so good to be in a permanent location and not wandering around anymore. And she had so little, it would not take her long.

"Not until after we give you our gifts," Martin said.

"Gifts?"

"Yes, your wedding gifts from us," Jakob said, licking his fork. "So damn good."

She sat at the table, the butt plug making her uncomfortable, but she ignored it and began to eat her pancake. It had been at least six months since she'd made pancakes and she felt relief she still had the touch.

The last time she made breakfast was right before her father died. Damn! She didn't want to think of that right now. She was happy. She was living on a ranch, and she had not one, but two husbands.

Right now, her life had done a complete circle. But she still missed Rusty, the horses, and even some of those stubborn goats. She missed her old life but knew she would never return.

This was her life and she hoped it would be as good as she dreamed.

"Why are you looking so sad?" Martin asked.

Glancing up, she gazed at them.

"We're about to give you our wedding gifts," Jakob said, frowning at her.

"Thank you and I'm excited to see what you give me,

but I feel bad that I have nothing for you," she said, hoping that would distract them.

She still had the two thousand dollars she'd made by selling all the animals, but that was sewn into the hem of one of her old dresses. It seemed like a safe place if she ever needed the money.

"Darling, we weren't looking for a gift from you," Jakob said.

Martin shook his head and stared at her. "I think something else is bothering you."

The man was way too perceptive. With a sigh, she gazed at her men. "The last time I cooked pancakes was for my father. Right before he told me that he'd lost our plantation in a card game. I'm so happy to be married to you and to be here, but this morning I was reminded of home and how I lost everything. Including my dog, the horses, and even some ornery goats."

The men stared at her. Martin rose and came over to her side. He knelt and laid his hand on her arm. "I'm sorry, Blanche. But we're so glad you're our wife and that you're here with us."

A tear trickled down her face. "I know and I feel the same. It's just sometimes a memory will hit me and it's a reminder of everything I've lost."

"Understand," he said. "Sometimes it happens to me as well."

"Come on," Jakob said standing. "Let's go show her our gifts. You guys are making me all melancholy. Don't need that the first full day of our marriage."

One thing she was quickly learning about Jakob was that he didn't like to have to deal with emotions.

Martin squeezed her to him and she kissed the top of his head. She was finished eating and she stood and begin to stack the dishes. She was a wife now.

Naked, she carried the dishes into the kitchen and began to fill a pan with water to heat and wash the plates and forks.

"Aren't you interested in your wedding gifts?"

"Very, just let me get these on to soak."

Jakob grabbed her by the hand and pulled her toward the living room.

"Now, wife," he said.

She giggled.

When they were in the living room, he had a wrapped box sitting there waiting for her.

Sitting on the horsehair sofa, she took the box and rattled it. Nothing.

"Hmmm, what could this be?"

She tore into the wrapping and when she had the fancy paper off, she opened the box. With a gasp, she pulled out a gold locket necklace.

"It was my mother's," he said.

"Before I left Charleston, she gave it to me and said that my father had given it to her. She wanted my wife to have it. And now you are the owner of the locket."

"I'll put our babies' pictures in it," she said.

He grinned.

She opened it to see a picture of his mother and his father.

"Are these your parents?"

"Yes," he said. "They were very young."

Gazing at him, she threw her arms around his neck, her naked breasts pushing against his shirt. "Thank you. It's beautiful and it's so sentimental. This means a lot."

"Just don't lose it," he said.

"I won't. We'll pass this down to our son to give to his wife," she told him.

"I'd like that very much," he said, kissing her on the neck.

She leaned back.

Martin was grinning at her. "My gift cannot be wrapped or even brought in the house."

Taking her hand, he helped her stand and then pulled her to the door. When she saw that he was going outside, she resisted.

"I can't go out naked," she said.

"Yes, you can," he replied. "Our hands are gone on Saturday and Sunday. They don't come back until late tonight."

"Are you certain?" she asked.

"Yes, now, come with me," he said, pulling her through the door.

She followed him outside and they walked to the barn. The hay was tough on her bare feet, but she didn't say anything. If he gave her what she hoped he had, she was going to be ecstatic.

Once inside, he took her to a stall.

There was a beautiful palomino horse.

"This is Sweetie," he said. "She's yours."

Tears welled in her eyes and she gazed at the beautiful animal. "Sweetie. You're so beautiful."

She rubbed the horse's nose, letting the girl smell her hand, and the horse snorted and licked her hand.

"Oh my God, thank you, Martin," she said, crying as she threw her arms around him and kissed him. "I miss my horse so much from Charleston. I didn't know if I'd ever own another one. This makes me so very happy. Can we take her for a ride?"

"Of course," he said grinning at her. "But I think you should put on some clothes."

The man had no idea how happy he'd just made her.

She stepped out of his arms and rubbed the horse's neck. "I'll be right back and then we'll go for a ride."

Running into the house, she forgot about the hay sticking to her feet, the dishes, everything but the thought of riding her own horse.

Coming to Montana had been so hard, but maybe everything was going to be all right. She raced up the stairs and when she found her carpetbag, she pulled out her men's clothing.

For a second, she thought about Jakob and quickly decided she didn't care. She was not going to ride with a skirt pushed up around her legs.

Throwing the men's pants and shirt on, she grabbed her old boots and then ran down the stairs. She didn't have a hat, but she didn't care. She was going riding on her new horse.

When she reached the barn, the men had saddled three horses, including Sweetie, and were waiting for her.

"No. Just no," Jakob said, his eyes widening at the sight of her. "You're wearing britches. Men's clothing."

"I always wear britches when I ride," she said, not liking his tone one bit. The man could be so overbearing at times. And this apparently was one of those times.

Martin sighed. "We're here alone. No one is going to see her, what can it hurt? I think she looks rather desirable in those pants."

"My wife will always be a lady. I've ordered you a sidesaddle. I expect you to always wear a dress and act with decorum when you ride."

With a deep breath to calm her rapidly rising anger, she walked over to Jakob.

"I am a lady. I will always be a lady, but I do not have a proper riding outfit. I'm not going to wear a dress and show more skin than I would if I wore men's clothing. Riding with a sidesaddle is extremely dangerous as I've told you. I will never, ever, ride with a sidesaddle."

His face was red, and she could tell she'd made him mad, but she had her limits and he'd just crossed one. In a sidesaddle, a woman could so easily be thrown off. She was not going to take the chance. And besides, she'd have to ride slowly.

That was not going to happen.

The horses pawed the ground and she could see that Sweetie was ready to go. She'd been waiting patiently long enough.

"All right, you can ride in men's clothing today. But this week, we're going to take you to town and get you a woman's riding outfit."

The thought of wearing one of those pompous-looking outfits struck her the wrong way. "I'll choose the riding outfit."

He frowned and walked over to her.

"You're getting mighty saucy," he warned.

"I'm not about to wear some fluffy outfit that gets in the way and is dangerous. I'm not willing to fall off of a horse because my outfit got tangled up in my reins or saddle. You want me to appear a lady and I will do my best. But I will also be practical and not accept something just because it looks proper."

With a sigh, Jakob shook his head as he stared at her. She could tell he did not like her telling him what she would accept. Well, he would just have to get used to it.

"Let's go," Martin said.

A smile spread across Blanche's face as she reached into her pocket and gave Sweetie a bite of a carrot.

"Are you ready for our first ride together," she asked the horse. "I'm so glad you're mine. Now let's go."

She stepped up into the saddle and turned to see Jakob gazing at her his eyes dark with anger.

Her husband was not happy with her, but he would just have to accept that she was not going to always please him.

CHAPTER 17

*J*akob hurried up the stairs, his anger had simmered all afternoon and all through dinner while they sat outside for hours. The woman had defied his orders and must be dealt with.

Martin didn't feel the same way, but Jakob wanted to nip her independence in the bud before trouble started with her disobeying them. She was going to learn that disobedience would be punished.

He'd told her to go to the bedroom and prepare to be fucked that he wanted her ass sticking up in the air, her face head down.

Martin warned him. "I think you're overreacting. It's going to take a few days for us all to adjust. Don't be too harsh on her."

Just like Martin to let her off easily. Now would determine their relationship and he wanted Blanche to understand she was not going to get away with dressing like a man.

"She disobeyed me and you just want to ignore it? What happens when she disobeys and gets hurt? We're protecting her by making her face her disobedience."

"All this over her wearing men's clothes to ride? What's going to happen when something serious happens. Don't be too harsh on her."

Ignoring Martin, he hurried up the steps with him trailing.

When he reached the top of the stairs, he hurried into their bedroom and began to remove his clothes. Blanche lay in position at the top of the bed, her face in the sheets, her ass sticking up in the air.

Martin removed his boots, his pants, and his shirt. When the man finished, he crawled onto the bed beside her.

He rubbed his hand over her ass.

Damn the woman had obeyed him. Oh, how he wanted her disobedience. It would give him even more reason to spank her ass.

"Roll over and face us," Jakob said. He wanted her to experience some discomfort for not being the proper lady he wanted her to always be.

"What have I talked about from the time we met? What have I mentioned over and over?" he said, staring into her emerald eyes.

There was a fire burning there that he wanted to extinguish. A flame that he knew would always resist him.

He walked to the dresser where he selected a larger plug from the wooden box and a jar of ointment. "Work this plug into your ass. And then I'm going to spank you. You are not allowed to come."

Taking the plug from him, she put the ointment on the dowel and removed the smaller one. Slowly, she inched the plug in, breathing deeply pushing and pulling, she bit her lip as the fake cock popped into place.

All the while, she stared at Jakob like she was angry.

Well, she wasn't the only one.

When she finished, she tilted her auburn curls in one direction and narrowed her eyes. "You would have me wear a bulky dress and sit on a sidesaddle. Many women are injured riding that way. I know you want a lady and I'm doing my best to be one. But this afternoon, we were alone. What harm was it for me to wear men's clothing?"

He could feel his nostrils flare and he wanted to shout but lowered his voice.

"If I wanted to marry a man, I would have, but I want a woman to be my lady. And you'll be required to act as one. I will not accept you acting like a hooligan. I will not accept you wearing men's clothing on the ranch. You will always be a lady."

She tossed her auburn hair and glared up at him. "I'm not your mother. I'm not the lady she was, and I never will be. If you can't accept that, then we have no chance. But I will always act in public like a lady. Do you want me to act like a lady in the bedroom as well? Shall I remain cold and indifferent while you fuck me?"

Damn, the woman knew exactly how to get to him. No, he didn't want his mother in the bedroom. That was just gross. And no, he didn't want her not to react when they gave her pleasure.

Clenching his fist, anger filled him. "Enough talking. You're going to be punished. Across my lap."

She glanced at Martin and then crawled across the bed and laid across Jakob's lap.

"You're not being fair," she said.

He ignored her comment. "I'm going to give you five licks. Count them out loud. If you continue to sass me, you'll get another one."

"Have it your way," she said and glared at Martin.

The woman had such a stubborn streak. Today, she'd shown her spunky rebellious side and he expected his wife to obey him.

Gazing down at her white perfect ass, all he wanted to do was plunge his cock in her. To take her roughly from behind and show her that he was the man of the house. She was to obey at all times, but first, she needed her spanking.

"Do you agree that you deserved to be punished?" Martin asked her.

She bit her bottom lip. "No. What else did I have to wear besides my dress."

The sight of her wet, glistening pussy was almost more than he could bear. Her folds were shiny and slick and the urge to climb on the bed and sink into her was overwhelming.

Time for her punishment.

Jakob swatted her ass to give her a taste of what was to come, hitting the plug. She gasped and turned her emerald eyes on him, dark and filled with fury.

Leaning down, Jakob kissed her on the ass, running his tongue along the seam of her cheeks, the plug peeking out. "We're punishing you because you disobeyed."

Martin nodded and Jakob raised his hand and connected his palm with her rounded cheeks. A handprint appeared on her white ass.

"Lady one," she cried out her hands searching for something to grip onto.

Her words infuriated him. She was deliberately making fun of the fact he expected her to act like a lady.

Smack, Jakob hit her again.

"Lady two," she replied, her voice steady and firm.

Smack.

"Lady three," she said and it sounded like she was gritting her teeth.

Smack.

"Lady four," she cried.

A moan escaped from her.

To change the rhythm, he spanked her first rapidly and then slowly and methodically, taking care to make certain that her entire ass went from white to a blushing pink.

"Martin, make him stop," she cried.

"Enough, Jakob," Martin said. "You've made your point."

Tears were running down her cheeks, and for the first time, remorse filled Jakob. He'd gone too far in his pursuit of having a lady for a wife. And Blanche was suffering because of his delusional need for a proper woman.

Jakob pulled her into his arms and held her, rocking her. As much as he needed to and wanted to, Jakob couldn't find the words to apologize.

For five minutes, he simply held her and rocked her and let his guilt eat away at him. He'd been wrong.

Slowly Martin reached over and slid his fingers over her folds before he plunged them inside her. When he pulled them out, Jakob could see the wetness. "She's dripping."

"Darling, as much as you hate me right now, I think you liked that spanking."

"No," she said gasping. "It wasn't like the other night when you gave me pleasure. This time you were angry with me and no one likes that kind of spanking. Why is it so important that you have a lady as a wife? Why can't you just accept me for who I am?"

Why was he so obsessed? Because he was crazy.

"Because I...I want my wife to be completely opposite of the whores I use to frequent. I want the mother of my children to be as good as my mother."

Tear-stained cheeks, her dark emerald eyes glared at him.

"Don't you believe that I'm a lady? Wearing men's clothes does not make me any less of a good woman."

She was right, but it would hurt his pride to admit that he had been wrong.

Martin gave him a look that said *she's right and you're wrong.* Why did it feel like they both were upset with him?

"Maybe I should demand that you be the perfect gentleman. That you handle yourself in a certain way. And if you step out of line, I'm going to spank you," she said.

A chuckle came from him and he lifted her up and

kissed her smart mouth. His tongue demanded entry and he gave her a kiss that soon had her moaning.

That was what he wanted to hear. Not her sniffles or witness her tears. He wanted to have her moaning with need for him and Martin.

She pushed back and gazed at him. "Don't think that everything can be solved with a kiss."

"But I can try," he said as he laid her back on the bed and she spread her legs wide.

"And I can…" she gasped.

Jakob reached down and begin to play with her clit.

"Darlin', your pussy is so tight," he said as he leaned down and placed his mouth around her taut nipples.

Martin moved to her head and he pushed his cock toward her lips. "Suck me, Blanche."

She placed her lips around his cock, unsure of what to do.

"That's it, suck the head."

The walls of her pussy clenched Jakob's cock and his fingers played with her clit as he shoved into her over and over.

He couldn't wait until they both could claim her. He couldn't wait until she realized that he really only wanted to make her happy, though he was doing a lousy job of showing her.

Again, he needed to try harder. He needed to show her that he would always be there for her.

"Are you ready to come?" he asked her.

She nodded as Martin's cock still filled her mouth.

"Come when I tell you," he said, wondering if she could

last that long. With stroke after stroke, he felt his blood building.

"Now," he said.

With a last thrust, he coated the inside of her pussy with his come. She was his and Martin's, and he had to learn how to be a better husband to her. He needed to trust that she would always be a lady.

Martin suddenly pulled his cock from her mouth.

"Up on your knees. I want to fuck you from behind."

After Jakob slid off her, she rose onto her knees.

She glanced back at him and narrowed her eyes.

"Don't slap my ass," she hissed. "It's still throbbing."

Jakob's heart sank. He'd hurt her and he hadn't meant to do that. He would never intentionally hurt a woman. Especially one he was beginning to have feelings for.

"How about if I rub it to make it feel better," he said.

"That would be all right," she told him.

"Good. Move faster," he said. "I can't wait for your pussy to grip me again."

Martin spread her legs; her pussy glinted with moisture in the light.

Shoving two fingers in her, she moaned and raised her hips to meet his every stroke.

"Are you ready for my cock?"

A moan came from her. "Yes. Hurry."

Why hadn't she asked Jakob to hurry? Because Jakob had hurt her, and now it would take some time to build back her trust.

Martin plunged into her, and she groaned as he rubbed her on the ass and pulled her onto his cock.

Jakob knew he would die protecting his wife and Martin would as well. But Jakob had to control his need for dominance.

Pulling her head up, Jakob kissed her on the lips and she moaned as Martin drove his cock deep into her pussy.

"Don't come until I say you can," Martin commanded. "Or I'll enjoy shoving that butt plug in your ass."

A whimper came from her and Jakob could see she was fighting to keep from coming.

"Now," Martin said. "We'll come together, now."

One last shove pushed her over the edge and she cried out as Jakob held her in his arms.

"That's it," he said, watching her face contort, her emerald eyes darken with passion.

The three of them collapsed onto the bed and she took Martin's hand in hers. "Thank you."

Jakob was holding her in his arms. "I owe you an apology."

She turned to face him, her emerald eyes glimmering with tears.

"You're right. I need to know that you're a lady. And I punished you harder than I meant to. That's not right. It will never happen again."

Martin shook his head.

"Wow, I don't think I've ever heard you apologize before."

Blanche reached out and touched his face. "Apology accepted. Don't ever spank me that hard again. But I also have to tell you, that I'm probably not a great lady. You see, Mrs. Newton taught me before I left to come to Montana.

Being raised by my father, he had no idea how to make me into a woman or a lady. That's why they called me the wild child. I raised myself."

Astounded, Jakob stared at her. The woman he'd married was not a lady after all. He had two choices. He could accept her or he could walk away, and at this moment, he knew what he wanted.

He wanted Blanche.

"I like the wild woman," he said. "I promise you I'll curb my expectations. I'll do better. Just don't push me too far."

She grinned at him. "Thank you. And I'll try to be the lady that you want."

CHAPTER 18

Martin hated this day. Every year when it rolled around, he tried to keep himself busy or even drown himself in a bottle. But this year, he couldn't get drunk. It would upset Blanche and he couldn't disappoint her.

All day, he'd stayed in the barn away from the house, doing his best to avoid her and even Jakob.

It was best if he was alone, though the guilt ate at him like a lung sickness, and some days, he thought it would be better if he died. Then he would not have to live thinking about all the people who were not here because of him.

If only he'd been stronger and more demanding. If only the foreman would have listened to him. But those were wishes that could be changed.

Blanche waltzed into the barn and smiled at him.

"What are you doing?"

"Cleaning stalls," he said as he watched her go to Sweetie and give her a carrot. The woman was obsessed with her new horse, and it made him feel so good that he'd given her a gift she really wanted.

"Why are you so quiet today?" she finally asked. "I know something is wrong because normally you bounce in and out of the house, eating the cookies I'm baking or just coming in and kissing me. But you've not come in today."

He didn't want her sympathy. He didn't want to gaze at her and see the pity in her eyes. That's not want he wanted or needed. He just wanted peace. A peace to remember that this was the day his life changed forever.

This was the day the mine collapsed, killing over twenty people. Friends, family members, and even some of his cousins. This was the day he ran from the crashing walls and dust as fast as his feet would carry him.

"I'm not going away until you tell me," she said.

"I have no doubt," he replied, knowing she could be stubborn and persistent.

He hadn't gone to the cemetery today, and usually at some point, he put flowers on his parents' grave.

"I'll saddle Sweetie and we'll go for a ride," he told her, his heart heavy.

Running into the house, she soon returned. But this time she wasn't wearing britches, but rather a skirt she had made into a riding skirt. She had taken one of her dresses and sewn the skirt into two big pant legs, so when she stood, it looked like a dress. Hopefully, Jakob would approve.

Though Martin didn't really care. Where they were going, it was doubtful anyone would see them.

"I'm ready," she said, running into the barn breathless,

her long auburn hair flying behind her, her emerald eyes twitching with delight.

As much as he liked seeing her so happy, he didn't want to spoil their ride, and yet he felt it was time she learned the truth about him. Not that he wanted to tell her, but there were days when he couldn't put the past out of his mind. And today was that kind of day.

She stepped into the saddle, and he climbed onto his horse.

"Let's go," he said.

"Where are we going?"

"You'll see," he said and they rode along silently.

"What a beautiful day," she said, raising her face to the sun.

And it was. It was perfect with clear blue skies, a light cool breeze, and the sun shining brightly. Only his soul was dark and morbid on this day.

"Yes," he finally said. When he felt like this, he was never talkative and she seemed to sense from him that he didn't want to speak but rather ride.

They rode down the road almost to town. Just before they reached Treasure Falls, he turned down the lane to the cemetery. Sweetie followed him and soon he could see the sign, Treasure Falls Graveyard.

Blanche didn't say a word as they wound through the grave markers until he saw the one he wanted.

Made from a big rock, his parents' names were carved in the stone. Tears welled in his eyes, and he missed them as much today as he had all those years ago.

"Your parents," she said with a gasp. "They died on this day."

He stepped down from his saddle and then turned to help Blanche down from her horse. Together they walked up to the grave and he laid out the flowers he'd brought – wildflowers he'd picked earlier in the day.

"Yes," he said softly. "The mine accident occurred this day and they perished inside the mine. They died together. We found their bodies holding one another and that's how we buried them."

A special casket had been made to hold both bodies. He and his brothers had not had the heart to break them apart, so this was how they would spend eternity. In each other's arms.

"What happened," she asked quietly.

The wind blew a soft breeze through the cemetery.

"Two weeks before the mine collapse, I noticed there was a new crack that ran from the floor of the mine to the ceiling. At the time, it was my first year working in the mine shaft. I said something to my father, who told me to go to the foreman. That I was now an employee and I should be reporting to the right person."

Oh God, how he wished he'd made his father go with him to see what he found. That was probably his biggest regret. If his papa had seen the crack, then he would have immediately had them put in supports to keep the walls from crumbling. If only the foreman had given him some attention, but he just thought he was a young kid. The owner's son who didn't know shit.

"What did you do?" she asked.

He sighed when he thought about how the foreman treated him. "When I went to him, he laughed and said that crack had been there for years. It was nothing. Told me if I was going to be a miner, I needed to learn not to be so afraid."

"What happened," Blanche said, coming over and touching him on the arm as he stared down at the graves.

"Once a month, my parents came down to the mine to thank the miners for their hard work. My mother would bring them something sweet she made. It was their way of being close to the workers. Papa hated it when mother went into the mine with him and asked her to wait outside, but on that morning, she told him no. She was going in with him. Why she did this, I will never understand. But she went in with Papa."

A hawk flew overhead calling out its cry, searching the land for rodents.

"Where were you that morning?"

"Working in the mine. I got a huge splinter in my finger. More like a small stick. The foreman insisted I go up and let the doctor remove the splinter and bandage the wound to keep out infection. He laughed and said my papa would never forgive him if I lost a finger or a hand because he made me keep working.

"I made it ten yards beyond the crack when I heard the rumble. I started to run toward the inside, screaming for everyone to get out. When the crack widened and went all the way down the walls. The beams could not support the shifting rock and from the back forward the main tunnel began to collapse."

He closed his eyes, the memory of that sound almost like the emptiness that filled his soul as he thought about that day.

"Did anyone get out?"

"Only the ones that were close to the entrance like me. There were five of us, the rest perished behind the wall of rock that closed the mine. It took five days to dig them out, and by then, they had all died, including the foreman who refused to listen to my concerns. The man who thought I was just a kid and had no idea what I was talking about."

Suddenly she threw her arms around him, and he could feel her tears on his shirt. "No wonder you hate this day. No wonder you got out of mining."

His throat clogged with tears as he remembered stepping out into the sunshine, all covered in dust. The way it seemed like the earth was moving and the mountain was reclaiming the tunnel they had created. Of how after everything stopped moving, the men sprang into action and began to remove the rocks while others shouted for more beams to support the roof. How he knew, as he gazed at their panicked faces, that he would never see his parents alive again.

"It's my fault," he said. "I should have been stronger against the foreman and demanded they put in more support beams."

"Do you really think that would have stopped the mine from collapsing?"

Over and over, he'd considered if more beams would have stopped that rumbling noise. He didn't think it would have made a bit of difference. The mountain rained rocks down on them that day. The crack was just an indication of the bigger problems in the mine.

Even his brother believed that portion of the mountain was unstable and did not reopen that mining operation but moved to a new section of the mountain. A new place where they found the silver, crystal, and minerals they were searching for.

"No," he said softly.

"So why is this your fault?"

"I could have done more to stop the collapse. I could have made them listen to me."

"How?"

Lifting his hand from around her back, he ran it through his hair. "I just think there is more I could have done."

"You would have needed a miracle," she said. "The foreman refused to listen to you. He thought you were too young. How could you have gotten through to him? As much as you loved him, even your own father was not too concerned and didn't come look at the crack. When we don't pay attention to one another's concerns, it can cost us so much."

It was true that even his father had left it up to the foreman.

"It would have been so much easier if I'd died inside there with them," he said softly. "A lot less pain. A lot less sorrow. I've often thought of ending it all just because of the mine collapse. It would be easier."

Blanche glanced at him and shook her head. "Oh, hell

no. You lived through that hell for a reason. God has a purpose for you. You're going to be a father soon and your children do not need you to decide you can't live any longer with the pain. Those people who died in that mine accident would want you to continue living the life that was taken from them. It wasn't your fault. If you must place blame, then it's the foreman's for not listening to you. But don't you even think about leaving me behind with Jakob. We need you, and our children will need you. I need you."

The hawk circled above them as the wind whispered through the trees.

He glanced at Blanche and could see the concern in her bright emerald eyes shining with tears.

"Promise me, you'll not leave me," she whispered, her voice choking. "Promise. If I were one of those miners and I knew you killed yourself because of our deaths, I'd be angry. You're giving up your life and they had their lives taken from them."

He'd never thought of it that way, but maybe it was true. Maybe he needed to live his life for them. For all the ones who died because no one believed him. If only someone had listened to him, they would all be here.

Oh God, how he'd tried to convince that foreman, but he refused to listen.

He lifted his head and pulled Blanche deeper into his arms and kissed her, his lips covering hers, commanding her surrender. This was the life he was being blessed with. This woman was his wife and he hoped they would have children in a year.

She broke the kiss and stared into his eyes. And he knew she demanded that he give her his promise.

With a sigh, he closed his eyes. "I promise I will never leave you because of my own selfish actions. What God has in store for me, I can't commit a promise on. But if I die, it will never be from my own hand."

She grabbed his face and kissed him hard. "Thank you. You've carried a heavy burden for so long. Don't you think these people lying here in this cemetery would want you to be released from the guilt you feel? They know you tried to save them. They know it wasn't your fault. They want you to live a happy life."

"Maybe," he said, trying hard to believe what she was saying. It was just so different than what he'd believed all these years. But to live his life for them was an idea he liked.

"See that hawk up there. Give your guilt to him and let him carry it away. Be free to live your life without the burden of something you could not control. Even your mother and father would not have wanted you to suffer for so long from this tragedy."

Tears filled his eyes as he gazed at the hawk and slowly let his guilt fly away with the bird. Maybe it would come back. Maybe it would awaken him in the night once again, but for now, he felt lighter. Freer.

And he had this beautiful woman to thank for this second chance at life. A life without pain and guilt.

CHAPTER 19

*S*everal days later, Blanche pulled the last batch of cookies out of the oven. Today, she was meeting the ladies in town to say good-bye to Rose and Alice. They were going to make that long arduous journey back to Charleston.

And frankly, she was glad to see Alice go. The woman had not been nice to her and, in fact, hated her for some reason she had yet to learn.

Unable to accept having two husbands, they were returning to the city that she loved and missed. Everyone was gathering for their sendoff, and Blanche had made cookies to give to each one of the ladies. And a special going away gift for them.

They had endured a harrowing journey together and they all had a special place in her heart, except for Alice. And then, Blanche felt sorry for the woman. She obviously could not open her mind to the idea of two husbands and she didn't know what she was missing out on.

For Blanche, she loved her life with her husbands, and knew that in the days since their marriage, she was falling in love with them. She was waiting for the right moment to tell them her feelings. And she hoped they felt the same for her.

Today, Jakob and Martin were not quite certain they were ready to see her ride into town alone, but Blanche had absolute confidence. Plus, she wanted to show the ladies her wedding gifts: the horse she loved named Sweetie and the gold locket from Jakob.

"Let one of us go with you," Martin said.

"No, gentlemen, you have things that need to get done around the ranch. It's branding time, and since I can't help, I'm going to go see my friends. I'll be fine."

Jakob shook his head. "I'm with Martin, I think we should go with you."

"I'll only be gone a couple of hours. If I'm not home by dark, then you can get worried. But I think Sweetie knows the way home probably better than I do. And I really want to visit with the girls while none of my men are hanging around making me feel like I need to go."

Martin sighed and Jakob shook his head. "If you're not home by four o'clock, I'm coming after you."

She kissed him on the cheek. "I'll be fine."

Then she gave Martin a kiss. "In fact, after dinner tonight, I'll be ready for the both of you."

"Really?" Martin asked.

"Yes, I put the last butt plug in this morning. I think by tonight, you'll both be able to claim me at the same time," she said, knowing that would satisfy them and give them something to think about all day while she was gone.

"All right," Jakob said. "But be careful."

"I will," she promised and stepped into the stirrups, her new split-dress covering her legs properly. She smiled at Jakob. "I modified this dress so I could wear it when I rode. I'm trying to please you."

A smile spread across his face. "Thank you. It looks perfect. Now be safe and get back home."

"I will," she said and tapped the sides of Sweetie.

The horse promptly moved down the drive toward the lane that would take them into town. She gave her free rein and smiled as she enjoyed the countryside. It had been only days since the wedding and she couldn't be happier.

It seemed the three of them were growing closer, and as she turned to wave at them, her heart leaped into her throat. She loved them. Since her arrival in Treasure Falls, her feelings for each of them had grown.

Jakob was a strong man who wanted the world to know he could defend his wife and family. He wasn't afraid to stand up to anything. And his need for the perfect woman had almost gotten him into trouble. But somehow they seemed to have worked through his issue of needing a lady.

Since the night he spanked her, he had grown more tender and loving, and she believed he truly regretted letting his desire for perfection overcome his common sense. After she'd been honest and told him that she had only recently learned how to be a lady, he seemed to have settled down.

Now she felt like he would protect her regardless of whatever happened.

And Martin, her heart seemed to automatically connect with his in a way she never expected. Now she understood his moodiness, and since he told her what troubled him, she had helped him learn to smile more.

Truly, her life seemed almost perfect and she hoped it was that way for the other ladies she was meeting today. Riding Sweetie, they pulled up in front of Doctor Sanders's home and she gazed at the big house and smiled.

It was here that her life seemed to have come together. It was here that she married her men and dedicated her life to making them happy.

Sliding down off the horse, she pulled the boxes of cookies out of her saddle bags. Tying the reins, she smiled at the horse.

"I'll be back soon. Here's a carrot for waiting for me," she said and pulled one out of her dress pockets. The horse hungrily took the treat from her.

As she climbed the stairs, she hurried, eager to see the other women.

The door opened and Aunt Grace greeted her with a kiss on the cheek.

"You look so wonderful. Are you happy?"

A smile spread across her face. "Yes, I am."

"I'm so glad," Aunt Grace said. "The other girls are sitting in the parlor. I've had the cook fix lunch."

"Thank you," she said.

She hurried into the parlor and there she saw most of

the women she'd traveled so far with. "Ladies, it's so good to see you."

"Sit down," Daisy said. "We're talking about marriage and if we like it or not."

"Yes, join us," Mary said. "I'm wondering when the first one of us will announce we're with child."

Alice sat across from her and glared at her. "I thought you were already pregnant. Especially after you were so sick while we were on the trail."

Blanche wanted to spend time with her friends. She did not want to engage with Alice. So she ignored her.

For the next thirty minutes, the women caught up with one another, their laughter filling the house, while Alice did nothing but stare at Blanche. She said very little.

Finally, Aunt Grace came in and said it was time for lunch. They all stood and strolled into the dining room where they continued to chat over their meal.

All the time, Blanche had an odd feeling when she looked up and caught Alice glaring at her.

After the meal, they returned to the parlor where finally, Blanche stood and opened her bag. "I brought cookies for all of you." She handed out the small tins of cookies and gave Alice and Rose two tins. "I thought that maybe you might enjoy them on the return trip," she said.

Alice threw the tins at her. "I'm not eating your cooking. You're trying to poison me."

The women in the room gasped and it became quiet as they stared at each other.

Blanche no longer had to put up with Alice's condescension and ugliness. She'd come here today and even tried to be friends with the woman, but no more.

"Why do you hate me so much? Why do you tell lies about me? Have I done something to harm you?"

The woman stood and approached her. She grabbed the locket around her neck and yanked it off.

Blanche gasped, her hand going to her chest where the missing locket once resided.

"Yes, you stole my necklace. Your mother ran off with my father. Your family has done so much harm to mine. I only came out here with the chance for revenge. And I almost succeeded when you were sick. I thought that I gave you enough poison, it would kill you, but I failed. This time I'm not going to fail."

The women gasped as Alice yanked Blanche up from the couch.

"Give my locket back. My husband gave it to me. It's been in his family for generations. Inside is a picture of his parents."

Alice's fist flew and Blanche stumbled from the first blow to her face. It had been many years since Blanche had really fought. The last time had been in the schoolyard when someone said that her mother was a whore.

Alice came at her again, but this time Blanche raised her arm, blocking the woman's punch. Alice copied her move, but Blanche went beneath her upraised arm and punched her in the face. The woman retaliated and kicked her, but Blanche was not giving up. She rammed her fist into Alice's stomach and watched her stumble backward.

"Hit her again, Blanche," Daisy cried.

"Give me back my necklace," Blanche said, her focus on the woman.

"Never," Alice said almost breathless. "Come and get it."

In some ways, Blanche's skirt made it easier for her to maneuver around Alice and she swung again and hit her in the face. Blood spurted from Alice's nose and she grabbed it, beginning to cry.

Just then Aunt Grace walked in and gasped.

"What is going on?"

Blanche returned to the couch and cradled her eye where Alice had landed a blow. She would have a black eye and Jakob would probably send her packing. Ladies did not fight. Even if it was to save the necklace he gave her. His family heirloom.

"Give me back the locket," Blanche said.

"Never," Alice said, growling at her.

"Ladies," Aunt Grace said, coming to stand between them. "This is not appropriate."

No, it wasn't and Jakob would be so upset with her. She had tried so hard to be the lady he wanted and she'd failed.

"Open it and see who is inside. Because when you see it's not your locket, my husband will be the next person who descends on you. Those are his parents."

Shaking, Alice opened the locket and gasped.

"Told you so," Blanche said, leaning back.

Then she sat straight up. "Wait a minute. You said my mother ran off with your father. I've never heard this story. How do I know it's true?"

Alice glared at her. "How could you not know what she did?"

"My father didn't talk about my mother. I was very young when she left us."

Alice all but growled her face contorted with rage.

"Your mother ran off with my father and it destroyed my mother," Alice said, gazing at Blanche like she was a tramp. If she could get around Aunt Grace, Blanche was certain Alice would try to hit her again.

"I don't believe you. You were wrong about the locket. You're wrong about my mother," Blanche said, thinking it couldn't be true. Yes, her mother ran out on her father and her, but not with someone in town. Certainly, her father would have told her the truth. "Give me proof."

Alice's face turned red and she stammered. "My mother said it was your mother. Said she stole my father from her. My father took money, and together, they left to go to New York."

Blanche had always known that her mother deserted them. She remembered her leaving and how upset her father had been, but she hadn't known the details.

"If this is true, why am I to blame for this? I had nothing to do with it. My father refused to talk about my mother. You can't prove this and I don't know what happened. Why would you go after me?"

The woman seemed to pause for a moment, and she licked her lips uncertainty filling her gaze. "I wanted to avenge my mother. She died a bitter old woman and it's your family's fault."

Blanche could feel her temper rising. "What if I decided that your father was the one who lured my mother away and I came after you. Do you see how ridiculous this sounds? We were children. We had no control over what happened in our lives. Believe me, I have been so angry that my mother could go off and leave me. You had your mother to raise you. I did not. I had my father, but you lost yours. Why would you blame me?"

Alice's bottom lip trembled, and she rushed toward Blanche. But Aunt Grace stepped in between her, stopping her.

"Because your mother ruined our family."

Blanche had heard and seen enough. The other women were all staring in horror at them. "I'm sorry this happened to you, Alice. But I don't know if it was my mother who ran off with your father. Why don't you think about blaming him if you need someone to blame? I had nothing to do with this. After all, I was a victim too. Now, if you'll excuse me, I'm going home. Give me the locket back or my husband will come find you."

"Tell him to come and get it. I'm not giving it back. It looks just like the locket my father bought and gave your mother."

How could she explain this to Jakob? How could she tell him that Alice had taken the locket from her and refused to give it back?

"Fine," she said and suddenly she wondered. "What did your father do for a living?"

"He had a wagon that he took around to homes selling kitchen wares."

Well, damn, maybe her mother did run off with her father. All she knew was that her father said she ran off with the pan salesman and Alice's father sold pans.

Turning, she walked out of the room, eager to get away. What had started out as a fun reunion had become a sad desperate scene she had to get away from.

Her friends walked out with her and she felt Daisy's hand on her arm.

"Are you all right?"

"Yes," she said, knowing that she wasn't. While part of her knew she shouldn't let the woman upset her, it was a missing piece of her that she couldn't explain and that frustrated her.

And she'd taken the gift that Jakob had given her. She'd failed him miserably and she so wanted to make him happy. She loved Jakob and wanted to be the wife he so desperately desired.

They walked outside, and when she reached Sweetie, she turned to say good-bye, and Mary hugged her. "Don't let this destroy the happiness you have."

That was the problem. Jakob was going to be so upset when he learned she'd gotten in a fight and had a black eye. How could she claim to be a lady when she got into a fist fight at the Sanders's home?

"I'll do my best," she said sadly.

"Be careful going home."

Climbing up on Sweetie, she still had over an hour before she had to be back. There was one place she could get answers. One place that had a legend that said someone could see the dead.

What if she tried to see her mother?

Clicking her heels against the mare's sides she hurried in the direction of the falls.

One quick stop and then she would head for home and her men.

Though she knew that Jakob was going to be so angry with her.

When she came to the turnoff, she pulled the reins and Sweetie took her to the pond. She swung her leg over the saddle and dropped to the ground. An eerie feeling was about the place, and she gazed around at the bushes to make certain she was alone.

When she saw nothing, she went to the water and gazed down.

"Mother, I've missed you. I've hated you, and I can't help but still love you. Show me your face and tell me if you ran off with Alice Burns's father."

She waited and nothing appeared. With a sigh, she sank to her knees. "This legend is a lie. It's not true. Oh, if only you could tell me what I'm supposed to believe. How could you hurt that family so?"

A fish splashed and she gazed at the water. There was her mother's face and she reached out like she wanted to touch her, but the water rippled.

"Mother," she said, her memories returning full force of how she'd loved her as a child. Tears welled in her eyes. "I needed you and you left me."

Her mother's face turned sad and she nodded.

"I have to ask. Did you run off with Alice Burns's father? She tried to poison me, she's so angry at how our family destroyed her life."

Her mother's mouth dropped open and then she closed it. Closing her eyes, a tear trickled down her mother's cheek. She nodded and Blanche knew that it was true.

"How could you?"

She mouthed the words, *I'm sorry*. Her mother might have said she was young and stupid, but Blanche wasn't certain.

What could she say in return? How she had hurt not only Blanche, her father, and the Burns family. What was left to say?

She glanced at the pond and her mother mouthed the words, *I love you*, and then she slowly disappeared.

Blanche said nothing in return. She couldn't.

Just then Sweetie let out a fearful screech. Blanche turned toward the horse and saw her worst fear coming toward her. A grizzly bear.

Sweetie turned and ran from the pond, leaving Blanche to face the bear coming straight for her.

Dear God in heaven, what did she do now?

CHAPTER 20

*I*t was well past four when Blanche promised them she would return. Jakob saddled his horse and Martin came out and began to saddle his.

"Somethings wrong," Martin said. "She would not deliberately be late. Not the first time we trusted her to go alone."

"Agreed," Jakob said, his fear growing with every passing moment.

Since they married, Jakob had fallen helplessly in love with Blanche. No, she wasn't the perfect lady, but she was his lady, and he worried something had happened. Since the night he spanked her too hard, he'd felt remorse and the two of them had grown closer.

They knew how to push each other's limits, and yet for some reason, he knew she would not have deliberately disobeyed today. Something was desperately wrong. And he was frightened she had not returned home.

Martin finished saddling his horse and stepped up into the mount.

"Let's go," Jakob said.

He'd never been in love before, and yet Blanche was all he could think about, dream about, and she made him see things from a different perspective. She made him a better man. She made him a loving man, and he realized he needed someone to help curb his control issues.

And he hoped that he made her a better woman.

"Be on the lookout. Maybe something spooked Sweetie and she's walking not riding."

"No, she's too good of a horsewoman to let a horse get away," Martin said.

They picked up the pace once they hit the main road, and while they were not racing, they were not moving slowly either. They had to find her.

"Damn, I'm worried about her," Jakob expressed. "Something must have happened."

"Me too," Martin replied. "I can't stand the thought of her being hurt."

"Me either," Jakob replied.

"She could be expecting our child," Martin said.

The thought of her being pregnant spurred Jakob on a little faster. It was too early to know, but still it was possible.

As they neared town, they saw a horse come racing toward them.

"Is that Sweetie?"

"Yes," Jakob said and galloped toward the horse.

Jakob grabbed Sweetie's reins and pulled her to a slow

trot. The animal's eyes were wide with fright and she even tried to fight him a little.

"It's all right, girl," he said softly.

They rode a few more miles toward town. Sweetie began to act nervous as they neared the turn off to the falls.

"Let's see if Blanche is at the falls," Jakob said.

Martin spurred his horse and suddenly he pulled up on the reins.

"No," he cried, grabbing his gun.

Gunshots rang out and Jakob turned the horse and headed back toward the trail to the falls.

"Martin?"

"Get the fuck out of here," he yelled and then there were more gunshots.

He heard a loud roar and knew immediately what Martin was facing.

Dropping Sweetie's reins, he spurred his horse toward Martin and hopefully a still living Blanche.

When he raced into the pool area, a big brown grizzly bear was on its back two feet. Martin fired another round of bullets and when the animal saw that Jakob was grabbing his rifle, he fell to four feet and turned and raced into the forest.

"Thank God, you came," Martin said.

"Where's Blanche?"

"Here," she cried, and he saw she had climbed a tree. Not the best thing to do with a black bear, but full-grown grizzly bears were too large to climb. Thank goodness she'd done the appropriate thing.

"Thank goodness," he said with relief. "We've been worried sick."

He swung his leg over the saddle and dropped to the ground. Martin and he raced to the tree, Martin still carrying his rifle.

"I've been so scared," she said, tearing up. "Have you seen Sweetie?"

"I'm hoping she's just outside of here, grazing on grass. That's where I left her," Jakob said.

Slowly Blanche climbed down and when she reached the lower branches, she dropped into Jakob's arms.

"I'm sorry," she said. "There's something I need to tell you."

A frown creased his forehead and he let her sink to the ground. Martin grabbed her.

"I've never been so frightened. I'm glad you're all right."

It was then that Jakob noticed that her right eye was all swollen and puffed like she'd been in a fight.

"What happened?" he said, reaching over and touching her brow.

"Ouch," she said and pulled back. She licked her lips nervously. "Jakob, I really tried to be a lady. I try to be a lady every day to make you happy, but today I got into a fight."

"A fight?" he said.

For the next five minutes, she told him what happened at the ladies' luncheon. "Alice tried to kill me on the way to Treasure Falls. She hates me, and in some ways, I can't blame her. My mother ran off with her father. That's why I came here to the pond. Here, I spoke to my mother and she admitted she ran off with Alice's father."

A heavy sigh came from Blanche and she began to cry. "If you want to send me away, I understand. The reason we got into a fight is that she stole your locket. She ripped it off my neck and refused to return it to me. I told her it was a gift from you, but she didn't care. She would not return it. She claimed it was a locket her father had bought for my mother."

Anger as fierce as that ugly grizzly filled him. He glanced at Martin.

"Take Blanche and Sweetie home," he said. "I'm going to town."

Then he glanced at Blanche. "I'm your protector. I'm your husband. I'm supposed to do all the fighting for you. Next time, come home and let me do my job. Let me fight your battles for you."

She threw her arms around him and cried. "I'm sorry. I feel like I've failed you."

"No, we're both still learning. But you depend on me now to take care of your battles."

"I will," she said with a sniffle.

"I'll meet you at the house," he said.

He stepped into the stirrups and threw his leg over his saddle. Grabbing the reins, he rode off.

"Come on, let's get out of here before that grizzly decides to return," Martin said, taking her by the hand. He pulled her up in front of him onto his saddle and then they rode out of the falls.

Sweetie was munching grass waiting on them. Martin took her reins and tied her to the back of his horse.

"I want to hold you in my arms. I've been so afraid that I was going to lose you this afternoon."

Blanche shook her head. "I would die trying to return to my husbands."

CHAPTER 21

*J*akob walked into the house unable to shake how close they had come to losing Blanche. That grizzly would have torn her apart. A shiver rippled through him.

Yes, he'd retrieved the locket from that bitch Alice. She wouldn't be bothering them any longer. And in fact, Aunt Grace warned her that one more episode and she would be on the streets before the coach arrived to take her home.

Thank goodness, she was leaving, going back to Charleston on the next stage. Jakob intended to make certain she got on that rattle trap. She was not staying in Treasure Falls.

All he'd thought about was Blanche on the way home. If he continued on this path, she would own his heart and soul. And then he would be so vulnerable.

And yet he knew he loved her. Today had proven that to him. Yes, she got into a fight, but it was because she was trying to retrieve a family heirloom he'd given her.

Every time he looked at her, his heart clenched with terror and his dick would harden. Part of him wanted to run out the door, jump on his horse, and ride away, and then Martin would give him that look that recognized Jakob was dealing with his demons.

Tonight he hoped they fucked them away because he was tired of fighting his expectations and reality. Blanche had done what she thought was necessary to save his family heirloom.

And that made him proud.

A whining noise whimpered from inside his shirt.

"Shhh, it's okay. We're almost home and you're going to love your new mama."

Tonight he and Martin planned to claim her together and he couldn't wait. When he reached the house, he ran up the porch. Pulling out his gift, the puppy licked his face. His heart warmed with love as he entered the house. Martin and Blanche glanced up.

"You're home," she said.

He grinned. He liked the way she said the word *home* like this was her place as well as his. Then she saw the puppy and her eyes widened.

"If you're going to stay and make this your permanent home, you need a dog."

She jumped up and ran to him and he pulled her into his arms. Squishing the little dog between them.

"Thank you, thank you," she said, crying as she rubbed behind his ears. "I've missed Rusty so bad. But now we have this little pup."

Reaching into his pocket, he pulled out the locket.

"She resisted giving it back, but I told her that my next stop would be the sheriff and she returned it," he said, thinking the woman was a total bitch to him, and he was glad Blanche had busted her nose.

"I'm so sorry," she said, tears rolling down her face.

He reached for her and gently wiped away her tears. "Let me fight for you."

She nodded. "It's just I had planned on giving it to our first born and the thought of someone stealing it overcame me."

A grin spread across his face. That was what he wanted, this locket to be handed down to his son or his daughter. And he intended on buying more jewelry for Blanche to give to their children upon her death.

And Lord, he hoped and prayed it wasn't anytime soon.

"I love that idea," he said. "Now who is going to protect you from having to fight?"

"You and Martin," she said.

Taking the puppy from him, she cuddled him in her arms. "What are we going to name you, little pup? You're so cute."

The dog proceeded to lick her face and she laughed. "Puppy kisses."

Setting him down on the floor, he promptly peed.

"Oh dear. You're going to need some training. Outside. Puppies go outside," she told him before going to the kitchen to get a towel to clean up the mess.

The puppy scampered after her and she smiled at him. Then she glanced up at her husband and smiled. "Thank you. The best gift ever."

Jakob's heart warmed. He loved this woman and knew she had made his life so much better.

For the next thirty minutes, they played with the puppy until his eyes began to droop.

"Time for bed," she told him.

Martin went to the barn and found him a box and she lined it with rags.

"Night, night, baby," she told him. The little dog curled up and was soon fast asleep.

With a contented sigh, Blanche held out her hand to Jakob.

He pulled her deeper into his arms and Martin sandwiched her between them. No, he had not wanted to get married, but now he was so damn glad they had found Blanche.

She glanced up at him and then turned to face Martin.

"Gentlemen, I'll be waiting in the bedroom, naked," she said. "I suggest you hurry along. Tonight you can both claim me at the same time."

Martin's eyes grew large. "We'll give you five minutes to prepare." She ran up the stairs, a giggle in her voice.

Martin frowned at him. "I want to commend you on how you handled her fighting. Frankly, I was happy she stood up to the woman."

"Thank you, I'm learning. But I swear, Martin, I'm falling so hard, it's crazy."

Martin gave a chuckle. "Me too."

"I can't risk losing her. What if next time we don't reach her before the grizzly attacks?"

A sigh came from Martin. "We need to teach her some

survival skills. After all, she could be here at the house alone or with our children. I think next week, she'll be learning how not to be a lady."

Jakob laughed. "She knows how to handle a gun. We need to teach her how to protect herself and the house. But instead of concentrating on how it will feel if something happens to her, I'm going to love her with all my heart and soul up until I take my last breath here on earth or she takes hers."

"Good idea," Martin said. "Now, let's go claim our wife. We've been waiting for days for this night, and finally, it's here. I'm going to tell her tonight I love her."

"I am too," Jakob said, thinking this was going to be such a great evening.

Martin hurried up the stairs and Jakob followed him into the bedroom.

Blanche sat naked on the bed. "First, I want to talk."

The men sank onto the bed beside her still fully clothed. Jakob was anxious to strip his clothes and claim his bride.

She licked her lips as tears filled her eyes. "First, I want to tell you thank you for being so understanding, Jakob. I know you want a lady, and I'm trying so very hard to be the woman you need. Also for bringing me Montana. That's what I'm naming our pup. And Martin, you are a strong and kind man. You deserve happiness. I want to be the woman who makes you happy."

Martin wrapped an arm around her. "I'm trying very hard to remember that I did everything I could to help them that day."

"Good," she whispered as she stroked his cheek.

"You're my lady," Jakob said. "And I will love you until the end of time."

A gasp came from her.

"I love you. I love both of you. You are my husbands and I can't wait for us to create the family we desire."

Jakob couldn't wait either. Suddenly, he wanted children. Babies to suckle at her breast, toddlers running in the yard, diapers, and clothes strung up everywhere.

Martin leaned over and kissed her soundly on the lips. "Blanche, I love you so much. You rescued me."

She caressed Martin's face. "We rescued each other."

She faced Jakob. "I love you, Blanche," he said. "Lady or not, you are ours until the end of time."

A big smile spread across her lips, her emeralds stared at him with the softest expression, shining with pure love.

She reached up and brought his lips down to hers and kissed him in a tender way that let him know he'd be crazy to walk away from her love.

"If I'm taken from this earth, it won't be because I wanted to go." She grabbed Martin's hand and looked between the two of them. "Our marriage is unusual, it's different from most, but I'm the happiest I've ever been in my life. Now, will one of you, please, fuck me."

The two men laughed, stood, and began to shed their clothes.

Blanche crawled up on the bed and took the position with her forehead on the bed, her ass in the air. Just the way her men liked for her to be positioned.

"This is it. Tonight we're going to claim you at the same time. You're ready," Martin told her.

"Will it hurt?"

"If it does, tell us. If we're doing it right, you should be begging us to take you," Jakob told her, knowing he wanted to make this the best sex she had ever experienced in her life. This woman understood him and he couldn't ask for anything more.

Martin slid beneath her, his lips covering hers, possessing her.

With her ass in the air, Jakob rolled her clit between his fingers, twisting the little nub of nerves. A groan filled the air and she pushed her ass back.

With a thunk on the end of the butt plug, he began to twist it, pulling it almost out and then putting it back in. She gasped as he assaulted her clit and her puckered rosebud together.

Finally, she broke the kiss and glanced back at him over her shoulder. "Jakob Moore, take me. And you too, Martin. You are my men, make me yours."

Martin lined up his cock at the opening to her pussy, his fingers spreading her wide. "Tonight is about pleasure. Tonight, I'm going to shove my cock in you as far as it will go."

"Oh, please do," she groaned.

"And then I'm going to take your ass," Jakob said as he grabbed a jar of lotion and rubbed it on his cock and around her little rosebud. He pulled the plug completely out, knowing they would never need it again.

She must be thrilled to be rid of those things and yet it served its purpose.

Impatiently he waited as Martin pushed his cock into her sweet pussy. As soon as he was fully inside, Jakob pressed his cock onto her ass. She turned and glanced at him over her shoulder.

"Fuck me, Jakob," she cried. "Fuck me hard."

Slowly his cock entered her rosebud spreading the opening. The walls squeezed him, resisting as he took her.

He slapped her ass. "Relax, Blanche. Let me in."

"I'm trying," she said. "The two of you are so big that you're stretching me wide."

"Just a little more," he told her, knowing that once he was in, she would be theirs. He felt her rectum stretch, his cock suddenly plunging inside between her walls.

"Aargh," she cried.

For a moment, he didn't move as he gave her time to adjust to the feeling of fullness. He loved the way the walls clenched his cock.

Then he felt Martin begin to move inside her pussy. Jakob pulled when Martin pushed. Soon they had a rhythm going and he could feel his seed building.

No, he wasn't ready for this to end. This night was theirs and he wanted to go slower but knew he couldn't.

He was not going to last long.

Reaching between her legs, he found her clit and pushed it against Martin's cock and she groaned.

"Darling, I'm not going to last much longer. Come whenever you're ready because I'm about to coat your pussy walls with my seed," Martin groaned.

Jakob knew he wouldn't last much longer either. With his hand, he slapped her ass cheeks once, and this time, she screamed as her orgasm tore through her. It was like an avalanche as they all three came at the same time.

Together. The three of them, as it was meant to be. Together. The three of them happily in love. He'd never believed he would have this kind of marriage.

As his seed spilled into her rectum, his heart overflowed with love for this woman and he knew he would never be the same. They all three collapsed onto the bed, their bodies entwined as they slowly returned to earth. When finally his heart had slowed and his lungs were functioning, he pulled Blanche into his arms. "I love you, Blanche."

"And I love you," Martin said.

"You are my life. My men. Can we please do it again?"

The two men laughed and Jakob knew that finally he'd found the home he'd been searching for with a woman who was his perfect lady.

CHAPTER 22

a year later, Blanche put the baby to her breast. She glanced down at Martin Jakob Sanders and her heart filled with love. How had her mother ever walked away from her? She would never understand how she left her for a man.

"Is he finished yet?" Jakob asked, looking over her shoulder.

"No, he's still sucking, his emerald eyes gazing up at me like he knows I'm his mama. And I am, sweet boy. I will protect you with my life if need be," she whispered to him before she kissed his forehead.

At almost two months old, their son was starting to grow and change and his personality was beginning to shine through.

"I get to hold him next," Jakob said.

"Hey, it's my turn," Martin said. "You held him at lunch."

She smiled at her husbands. "Why don't you each hold

him for just a few minutes apiece. He'll need to be changed and then he'll probably fall asleep."

The two men glared at one another. Neither one of them liked to change his diaper, but they would.

"Maybe next time, you should have twins, then we'll each have a baby to hold," Martin said.

She glared at him thinking she couldn't imagine two babies inside her. "Why don't you have the next one."

The men grinned. "You did such an amazing job. We couldn't have done it as well as you did."

"Thank you," she said, gazing down at their son and then up at her husbands. "I love you so much, and I can't wait until you can claim me again."

Their eyes brightened. "Us too. Soon."

"How about tonight after Little Britches is down. It's been two months. I think I'm ready."

The two men turned and smiled at each other. "You take the baby."

"No, you take the baby, I'm going to get the room set up."

Now that was different.

"Why don't one of you take the baby, so that I can get prepared. Once he's asleep, I'm all yours."

"Love you, Blanche," Martin said as he bent down and took the baby from her.

Jakob helped him by making certain that the baby's head was in the right place.

"I love you too, Blanche," Jakob said. "I can't wait to take you tonight."

"Me either," Martin said.

"Put the baby down, and then we'll go upstairs," Blanche said.

She couldn't help but think about what had brought her to Treasure Falls. She really should write the man who took the plantation away from her and thank him. Because of her trip to Montana, she had everything she wanted in life. Everything.

Just then Montana bumped her hand. She gazed down at the dog and rubbed him behind the ears. "I can't wait until you and Little Britches can play together. I know you'll look out for him."

Gazing around the house that was now her home, she knew that coming to Montana had been the best decision she'd made.

I ENJOYED these characters so much. They were so much fun to write and I hope you enjoyed them as well. In the meantime…Our Dangerous Bride is up next. Here's a little snippet.

FRANCIS NELSON SPURRED her horse faster, racing down the road. The posse was not far behind, and while part of her wanted to ride through the trees, one wrong move and you could lose your head.

Her horse was starting to tire and she hated that she was riding the animal so hard. But when the law was on your tail, you had to run.

"Come on, girl. We're almost to the turnoff," she said, knowing if she could just reach the hollows, they would never find her. She turned down the hidden lane and quickly took the trail that was the back entrance to the house. During the war, they had used this little hideaway often.

Slowing her horse, she reached the barn. Lather dripped from Sadie's sides. Jumping off, Francis rushed the horse to the inside of the barn, knowing they weren't out of danger yet. At any moment, the law could be closing in.

She untied her saddle and pulled out the sack of money. Not a lot, but enough to keep them from going hungry.

Her sister Lilly raced into the barn. "The law is riding up. Hide."

"Shit," she said. "Release Sadie and let her go free. I think I about ran her to death."

They released Sadie out the back of the barn and Francis slapped her on the hind end. The mare took off, but she wasn't running. The horse wasn't dumb and she disappeared into the trees.

Oh God, Francis hoped Sadie would survive because she loved that horse, but today, she'd given her all.

"Hide, they're at the house," her sister said urgently.

Francis opened the underground cellar door and slipped inside. Her sister covered the door with a blanket and then scattered hay.

"Miss Nelson," she heard a voice call.

"Back here," her sister said cheerfully. "I'm cleaning out the horse stalls."

Francis would be surprised if Lilly knew how to clean a horse stall. Between the two, her sister did more of the cooking. And none of the outside work.

The law had never gotten this close. Of course, as soon as she stepped out of the bank, it seemed like they were waiting for her. And the chase had been on. Racing through the streets, down the road, and out of town, she'd clung to Sadie fearing at any moment they would tumble and be captured.

If they caught her, she would surely hang because the law didn't give women bank robbers a break.

Stepping back as far into the depth of the cellar as she could, she heard three men walk into the barn.

"Where's your sister Francis?"

Lilly turned and smiled. "Who wants to know?"

"I'm Sheriff James Randolph and these are my deputies," a man said. "We need to speak to Francis. We think she's the person who's been robbing the bank."

Lilly started laughing. "You men been drinking? My sister Francis is one lazy woman. Why do you think I'm out here in the barn taking care of the horses? It's because she refuses to. Most of the time, she's in town having tea with some of the other women."

"Tell me which ladies," the sheriff said. "I want to verify she's having tea and not withdrawing cash."

Oh, very clever man. Francis had never attended a tea. The Nelson sisters were not invited. Since the war, they lived on the edge of poverty, their names were never mentioned when there was a party of any kind.

"I don't know who. If I did, I would tell them not to invite her. She needs to be here with the rest of us cleaning horse stalls, chopping cotton, canning, and doing the wash. Things a young woman should never have to do, but since Papa died, we're managing."

The man was silent for a few moments before his voice became gruff. "Look around out back and see if she's hiding."

"Do you know how to clean horse stalls, Sheriff?"

"Of course," he said.

"Well, if you're going to stick around then make yourself useful. I need to finish up and then tend to all that laundry hanging on the line. If that lazy sister of mine would stay home, all this work would get done."

Oh yeah, she was so lazy. She was the one holding up the bank so they had money to pay the taxes on the place and also put food on the table. Until the next harvest came in, things were going to remain tight.

Their fortunes had not improved.

"Sheriff," her mother called, "I think I found something you might want to see."

Her mother had no idea what was going on. Not long after their father's death, it was like she woke up in a different world every day. At night, she kept waiting for their father to come home. If Francis went to jail, she worried what would happen to her mother and sister. They were all barely surviving.

And Momma, bless her heart, continued to wait for their father to come home.

Lilly began to hum a tune while she cleaned the stalls. Acting like she didn't have a care in the world when so much was at stake.

Her mother's screams pierced the air. "Stop. Don't touch me or my husband will kill you."

Shouting came from outside and Lilly dropped the pitchfork and hurried from the barn. Sitting there in the darkness, it was all Francis could do to keep from jumping up and running out the door to see what was happening.

"You son of a bitch, what are you doing?" Lilly cried.

"Can't you see something's wrong with her? She's an old woman," Lilly screamed. "Leave her be. She knows nothing. She barely even knows she's here."

They were trying to draw Francis out of hiding. And it was working. Another minute of this and she'd come out fighting.

"You tell your sister this time we only tied up your mother. If she doesn't turn herself in within twenty-four hours, we'll harm your mother and you. We know she's the bank robber and she's got to pay for what she's done."

Normally, Lilly would have cursed them, but all Francis could hear were sobs. What was she going to do? She couldn't let them harm her remaining family. Maybe she should just walk out of the barn like nothing had happened.

But she was still wearing her men's clothing. They would easily recognize her as the bandit. If they caught her, she would hang.

"Get off our property," Lilly said. "And don't come back. My sister is not a bank robber. Now get out of here before I grab my gun."

Available at Your Favorite Retailer!

PLEASE LEAVE A REVIEW

Did you enjoy the book? Reviews help authors. I would appreciate you posting a review.

Follow Lacey Davis on Facebook.

Sign up for my New Book Alert and receive a free book.

The Gambler Takes a Chance on Treasure Falls

Peart Tuttle is the slyest gambler in town. For the last two years, she has survived on her own by making enough money to keep her from going broke. But now her gambler's luck has run out and she owes the saloon a hefty sum. Time to join the mail-order brides and get out of town.

Widower Anthony Sanders owns a ranch in Treasure Falls and believes he will never love again. Yet, he wants children to pass his land to. Wesley Pickens has led a reckless life and only recently with Tony's help has managed to stay out of trouble. Would a woman settle him down or will the bad boy return to his wild ways?

Can Pearl escape her debts or will the past make her pay up in her new hometown? Will Tony and Wesley put their histories behind them or will Pearl become the abandoned bride of Treasure Falls?

Available at Your Favorite Retailer!

The Princess and the Paupers

Carrie Spencer grew up in Treasure Falls with two fathers. When her parents were killed in a mining accident, she learned exactly why two husbands were essential. Now she's grown and ready for two men of her own. But there are no eligible men in Treasure Falls.

Levi Daly and Jasper Vanderbilt have traveled the world, made their fortune, and now want to return home. No longer are Levi and Jasper two poor kids, living on the wrong side of Main Street. No longer are they not good enough to marry a Spencer, or so Levi believes. He has loved Carrie since they were children, but Jasper and she were childhood enemies.

Can Levi convince Carrie to marry him and Jasper? Or will they continue to be enemies? Can the poor kids marry the town's favored daughter?

Available at Your Favorite Retailer!

Also By Lacey Davis

Blessing, Texas Series
Loving My Cowboys
Two Cowboys' Christmas Bride
Two Cowboys One Bride
Two Cowboys Too Perfect
Two Cowboys to Protect Her
Two Cowboys Save Christmas
Blessing, Texas Box Set 1-3
Blessing, Texas Box Set 4-6

Bridgewater Brides World
Their Perfect Bride
Their Tempting Bride
Their Scandalous Bride

Return to Blessing, Texas
Come Home to the Cowboys

Treasure Falls Brides
Our Fugitive Bride
Our Desperate Bride
Our Wild Bride
Our Dangerous Bride
Our Lucky Bride
Our Christmas Bride
Treasure Falls Brides Box Set 1-3
Treasure Falls Brides Box Set 4-6

Want to learn about my new releases before anyone else? Sign up for my New Book Alert and receive a complimentary book. Blindfold Me.

ABOUT THE AUTHOR

Lacey Davis is a pseudonym for a USA Today bestselling author who wanted to try her hand at writing sexy romance. With these novels, I hope to write sizzling romances that will leave you grabbing a fan to cool yourself off.

If you like hunky bad boy heroes who like to be in charge and strong pretty women who are willing to risk it all, then look no further. These sexy reads will get you in the mood. Come experience strong women who will tame these bad boys and leave them wanting more.

The End

www.ingramcontent.com/pod-product-compliance
Lightning Source LLC
Chambersburg PA
CBHW071238170626
46809CB00015BA/2609